Timber Wolf

Timber Wolf

Caroline Pignat

Red Deer Press

Published by Red Deer Press, A Fitzhenry & Whiteside Company
195 Allstate Parkway, Markham, ON, L3R 4T8
www.reddeerpress.com

Published in the United States by Red Deer Press, A Fitzhenry & Whiteside Company
311 Washington Street, Brighton, Massachusetts, 02135

Edited for the Press by Peter Carver
Cover design by Alan Cranny
Text design by Daniel Choi

Printed and bound in Canada

5 4 3 2

We acknowledge with thanks the Canada Council for the Arts, and the Ontario Arts Council for their support of our publishing program. We acknowledge the financial support of the Government of Canada through the Canada Book Fund (CBF) for our publishing activities.

Library and Archives Canada Cataloguing in Publication
Pignat, Caroline
        Timber wolf / Caroline Pignat.
ISBN 978-0-88995-459-5
        I. Title.
PS8631.I4777T54 2011   jC813'.6   C2011-905853-7

Publisher Cataloging-in-Publication Data (U.S)
Pignat, Caroline.
        Timber wolf / Caroline Pignat.
[224] p. :   cm.
Summary: Jack Byrne, eager for adventure, sets out into the Canadian wilderness to prove himself, but instead wakes up alone, injured and completely lost with no memory of what happened, how he got there, or who he is. At the same time he meets, is terrified by, and eventually guarded by a young wolf who appears out of the woods early in his ordeal - and also stumbles into a relationship with an aborigi-nal family whose young son's own stormy coming of age coincides with Jack's developing awareness.
ISBN: 978-0-8899-5459-5 (pbk.)
1. Adventure fiction – Juvenile literature. 2. Adolescence -- Fiction. I. Title.
[Fic] dc22   PZ7.B546Ti   2011

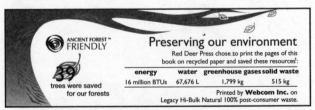

Preserving our environment

Red Deer Press chose to print the pages of this book on recycled paper and saved these resources[1]:

	energy	water	greenhouse gases	solid waste
	16 million BTUs	67,676 L	1,799 kg	515 kg

39 trees were saved for our forests

Printed by **Webcom Inc.** on Legacy Hi-Bulk Natural 100% post-consumer waste.

[1]Estimates were made using the Environmental Defense Paper Calculator.

FSC
www.fsc.org

MIX

Paper from responsible sources

FSC® C004071

For the strength of the Pack is the Wolf,
And the strength of the Wolf is the Pack.
– Rudyard Kipling

For the Crannys, Jacksons, Flemmings, and Pignats.

My pack.

CHAPTER 1

The howl wakes me, calls me from one darkness to another. My right eye opens but my left is a throbbing slit. Bare branches. Twilight beyond. I'm on my back. Outside. Somewhere. I'm alive. Barely.

What happened?

My head pounds. I raise my hand to it but my frozen fingers feel nothing. Their grazed and swollen knuckles tell me numbness is probably a blessing. Was I in a fight? I roll onto my side, gasping small clouds of steam as pain stabs my ribs.

How long have I been lying here? A thin layer of snow covering my legs shifts as I move. Bruised, but not broken, thank God.

Sitting up, I blow into my hands. The heat of it stings my reddened fingers and I shove them into my pockets, surprised to find a pair of woolen mittens that must be mine. I slip them on. Shivers wrack my body. Whatever happened to me, it hasn't killed me, but sitting in this frigid snow surely will.

Standing takes more effort than I expected. I stagger a few times and when I finally get to my feet, everything spins around me. Gripping a nearby birch trunk, I close my eyes and take shallow breaths. After a few moments, the spinning slows and I glance around the clearing. A gorge of sorts, with a fifteen-foot cliff rising up behind me and a mild slope ahead. A river bed, perhaps. Yet, none of it seems familiar.

"Hello?" I call. The yell clangs in my head like a spoon in an empty pot.

No tracks lead in or out of the clearing. Not even mine. Odd. The dusting of flakes wouldn't have covered them completely. My boots crunch in the snow as I turn.

Surely, someone is looking for me. Must know I am missing.

"I'm here!" The ache in my side grows stronger with every breath. I don't want to yell again, but it might help them find me. Holding my bent arm tight against my aching side, I squeeze out the sound like an old bagpipe. "It's me, it's ..."

The steamy words dissolve before me.

Who am I?

Panic grips me. I look around for help but the oak, birch, and pine trees stand in cold silence. How is it I know their names, but not my own?

Slumping to the ground, I scan the wide sky as the cold

truth settles upon me. Lost, I am. Completely lost. I know neither where I am nor where I'm from.

Homeless. Nameless. Hopeless. Yet, try as I might, nothing comes to mind but the fat flakes drifting down from the endless winter black.

CHAPTER 2

"*Careful now,*" *he says. The glow of the fire flickers across his face as he gives me his knife. It seems huge in my tiny hands. How long I've wanted to hold this red wooden handle. To wield its metal blade like him.*

Night after night, I've watched. I know every curve of his hand, every scar, every callus. I can do this, for I've done it a million times in my mind. Setting the stick in the crook of my arm, I grip it just short of the whitened tip where he's started to whittle, hold the blade like he would. It glints in the firelight and I pause, flash it a couple of times. It feels good.

"I'm just like you, amn't I?" I say.

"That you are, wee man." He tousles my hair. "Go on now, give it a go."

I attack the wood with all my force. I'll show him how well I can do it. The blade bites into the bark and snags. I saw it out and try again, only to have it catch in another notch. This isn't how it's supposed to happen. I grit my teeth and try again, grunting as I push harder.

"He's too small," a girl's voice says from the shadows. Her laughter makes me want to take the knife and stab the stick into smithereens.

"Easy, boyo. 'Tis no ax for hacking. Gently." He moves his hands in that familiar motion as though he holds the stick and blade. His wrist rolls with the ease and strength of the tide. "Gently, now. Let it kiss the wood."

Taking a deep breath, I try again. I will do it. I will, bedad. I angle the blade along the stick and draw it up to the point. This time it doesn't hook. A small white curl begins to grow on the edge of my blade. The girl makes a kissing noise with every move of my knife. I tense at the sound and push harder. She giggles and continues until I can take her noise no longer.

"Hush up!" I yell, glancing at where she sits in shadow. But the moment my eyes leave the blade it slips and gouges my finger. At first, I feel nothing but a curious awe for the moon-shaped slit. But then the blood comes and, oh, the pain!

He's on his knees, cradling my hand, as he examines the cut. "It's a good one."

"Don't ... don't touch it," I whine, for surely my whole finger's about to fall apart like a sliced sausage. I feel dizzy at the thought. But he pinches the cut together between his strong fingers.

"I told you he was too small. He's only a baby," that girl says.

"Get a bandage, pet," he tells her, and she disappears.

Like magic, his touch lessens the pain. But I can't stop the tears. They burn and boil over, no matter how hard I try to keep them in, for I know I've disappointed him. I know he'll never let me touch his knife again.

"I can't do it like you do," I mumble.

"So, you made a mistake," he says, but there's no judgment in his voice. "You can let it beat you ... or build you."

I don't really know what he means.

"Did you learn anything?" he asks.

"Not to look away," I answer, for I'll not be doing that again.

"I did, too." He points at the familiar scar, a white sickle between his thumb and finger, and then at one more at the tip of his index finger. "Eventually." He chuckles. "I guess you're a faster learner than me."

The fire crackles behind him, outlining his dark form with an orange glow. Picking up the tiny shaving, he places it in my right palm. A tiny whorl of wood. Small, but perfect. I made that. I did it ... once. But I know I can do it again. Even better.

I want to tell him. To prove it to him. But before I can speak, he lays the small knife in my palm beside the shaving.

"This is yours, now," he says, glancing over my shoulder. He looks at me and folds my fingers closed over the worn wooden handle. "*Our little secret, right? Your mother'd only worry.*"

The girl returns behind me, hands him the bandage. "I knew you'd cut yourself."

"*I didn't do it on purpose," I say. "'Twas a mistake.*"

"*A foolish mistake," she adds.*

"*There's no such thing." I catch his eye and he winks. "As long as you learn from it."*

He keeps the pressure on my finger for a bit longer. My cut throbs, though I can't tell if it's his heartbeat or mine.

CHAPTER 3

I must have slept or passed out, for the dark sky is deeper now. The dream seems so true. I half hope that it is and that this is the nightmare, but the chills and aches in my body feel real enough. Too real.

Using the sapling beside me, I pull myself up and glance at the blackened sky. Even if they are coming, they'll not be here tonight. A search party would soon need one of their own, were they out on a starless night when the moon is but a sliver. All I can do is make some kind of shelter and wait until morning.

I rub my arms, mindful of the dull ache in my ribs, and check inside my coat. My shirt is dry. No blood—a good sign. Being alone, lost in a forest on a winter's night, is bad enough. I'm looking for all the good signs I can find. At least I have a heavy coat and scarf. A hat and mitts. Warm boots. Had I not, I doubt I would have survived this long, and they'd be finding a corpse and not a boy tomorrow.

I shiver as a cold winter wind bites through me. Warm coat or not, I have to find shelter. I scan the area. The best place seems to be against the rock wall just under the ledge. Drawing nearer, I notice the rock face is ridged like a bit of old bark, and one of the furrows seems just about big enough for me. I'd have protection from the cutting wind and snow. The starless sky makes me think there's more coming. Picking up a stick, I poke at the mound of leaves and twigs piled in the crook of the crevice. It seems I'm not the first creature to settle here. The nest is empty, but it gives me another idea. Even if I am sheltered from the wind and snow, a nest of my own would save me from the bitter cold.

I circle the area for pine boughs, careful not to lose sight of the cliff, my only bearing. The thin branches break after bending them back and forth a few times, but the bigger ones take more effort. Effort I don't have in me. Instead, I settle for the little ones. I have to stop many times just to catch my breath, for I'm wheezing like an old man. I still can't take a deep draw of air without that sharp pain in my side stopping me short. Being only able to manage four or five boughs at a time means many trips, but it's warming me, just the same. My fingers ache, but I try to celebrate the chilblains in their tips, for it means my blood is pumping. Another good sign.

What seems like hours later, I finally have a small pile of

boughs at the base of the ledge. Just enough to line the floor of the widest cleft in the rock with a few left over for coverage. I drop onto the lumpy pile, heedless of the twigs jabbing in my back. The work has exhausted me. I just want to sit, to sleep. But I fight the tiredness to drag the last few branches over top of me as I lie down. The needles prick my face, their pine scent heavy in my nose. Through the thin limbs, I can just make out the bare trunks and bushy firs standing guard in the silent dark.

My home might well be just past them or a short ways up the ravine. Maybe my family is there, waiting for me by the fire, wondering what's keeping me. No doubt, whoever they are, they'll tease me terrible if I've gotten lost in my own backyard.

I roll to my side, aware of something hard beneath me, against me, inside my coat. I pull off my glove and, reaching into my coat, feel the small lump next to my hip. But it's no branch. I know it, even in the night's darkness as I pull it out. I know it.

The red-handled knife. The one from my dream.

No, not my dream. From my memory. From my father.

"Da," I whisper, as though saying it makes it real.

But the same part of me that knows that man is Da, knows something else. Though I can remember neither who I am nor how I got here, something deep inside me, that knowing at the core, tells me that I am a long, long way from home. My side aches, or maybe 'tis my heart, but I won't give in.

For all I have lost and forgotten, I have two things. I have one memory. And I have Da's knife.

A good sign.

CHAPTER 4

I shiver in the harsh, morning light, wakened by the griping crows. It takes me a moment to remember where I am. The clearing. The bed of boughs. But I can remember no more. My body aches as I sit up, but 'tis the sharp pain in my side that has me most worried. I press against it and wince.

Broken rib? I can't be sure. One thing I do know is my hunger. I check my other pockets, hoping I'd squirreled away some food before I left from ... wherever. In them, I find a flint and a length of twine. I slip them back into my pocket. In the other side of my coat, I find a bit of bread. It's hardened around the edges but softens in my mouth when I slurp a bit of snow melted in my cupped hands. The morsel is just enough to goad my hunger. Still, the scrap of food gives me some hope. I can't be that far from civilization. Not with bread on me.

Standing, I try to draw a deep breath. My side protests and my nostrils soon freeze shut, but the chilled air carries neither hint nor hope of a loaf browning by any fire. There's no scent but the forest that sprawls as far my eyes can see. The sky spreads over me like a taut blue sheet. Yet from one tucked horizon to the other, I can find no thread of smoke upon it. If there is a cottage nearby, its hearth is cold. Maybe they're out looking for me. I wonder how long it will take. Noticing how last night's snowfall has buried any tracks I'd left in the clearing, I wonder how they'll ever find me.

A fire would help, I think, remembering the flint. *'Twill keep me warm, send a signal, and maybe even cook my breakfast. If I can find any.* My mouth slathers at the very thought. When my rescuers arrive, I'll invite them to stop and have breakfast with me. I smile to myself, thinking about how surprised and pleased they'd be. Whoever they are.

After spending the morning snapping and dragging more dry branches, my body aches and my head pounds. The pain in my side has grown much worse; every movement hurts. I'm panting like an old dog on its last legs and I haven't even started looking for food yet; I'm near dead.

I have my father's knife, but, sure, what good is it now? There's no way I can hunt in this condition. I can neither run nor throw, and even the deafest, dumbest hare would hear my haggard wheeze from a mile away. *A rescuers' breakfast?*

I scoff at my foolishness. *Never mind them ... what, in God's name, will I eat? And what if my rescuers don't come for some time?* Panic rises like bile in the back of my throat. But before it chokes me, it's quelled by the sight of a bit of green waving deeper in the woods.

In a spindly forest of naked trees, this brilliant shrub catches my eye. Leaving the last few bits of firewood, I edge deeper into the forest for a better look. I can no longer see the rock cliff I've been using as a bearing, but my footsteps are clear enough. Besides, it's not snowing, so I'll have no trouble backtracking.

The closer I get, the more berries I see. Small, red balls cluster in groups among the dark green leaves. Taking off my mitt, I pluck one and sniff it, roll it in my palm. It seems harmless. But why haven't the animals picked this bush clean like they did the others? My stomach grumbles. Surely one or two berries can't hurt me. I raise the tiny, red ball to my lips, but a crack and squeal nearby makes me jump and drop the berry.

I'd grown used to the sounds of the woods, the *fa-whump* of snow falling from branches, the snap of frigid twigs. But that was not a sound I'd heard before.

"Hello? Anybody there?" My words float into the deep woods and fade like steam.

I wield my knife, wave it before me. It won't do much good

against a wild animal, but I feel better holding it as my boots squeak and crunch with every step. Stopping to listen, I hear nothing more than my panting breath and pounding heart. I press on through the prickly fir branches, heading for the source of the strange sound. A flash movement catches the corner of my eye. There. Yes, something furry about shoulder level is definitely moving just beyond those bushes. I crouch among the boughs, unsure of my next move.

A rescue party would have answered my call. Whatever is shifting side to side beyond the branches isn't human. An animal, to be sure, but how big? My stomach grumbles, urging me onward despite how ridiculously small my knife seems in my mitted fist.

It's winter. Food is scarce. Whatever is on the other side of those bushes might be something I can eat.

My steps falter and I stand in the cold silence, for it occurs to me that whatever is on the other side of those bushes might be watching me and thinking the very same thing.

CHAPTER 5

If it hasn't run yet, then it doesn't know I'm here. Surprise is the only ammunition I've got, truth be told. I try not to think about the possibility that it's a bigger animal, a hungry animal, one that I can't outrun. I slip off my mitt and grip the knife's cold hilt in my sweaty palm.

This is it. Eat or be eaten.

My heart is racing and suddenly the pain in my side seems less. Like my body is getting ready for the attack. With a mighty battle cry, I burst through the bushes, face first, into the fur, fangs, and claws. Convinced I'm being mauled by some ferocious beast, I scream and frantically slash the empty air before tripping over my own feet and landing flat on my back. 'Tis only looking up that I realize that ferocious beast of fur and fang is nothing more than a dead rabbit swinging from a sapling. I sit up and glance around the thick woods, for I swear I heard a girl's scream during the attack.

I scan the area—nothing. No footprints, no movement in the timbers. I realize two things then. One: I'm well and truly alone. And two: 'twas me screeching. Red-faced, I jump to my feet and brush the snow off my legs. Thank God I'm alone. The last thing I want is for my rescuers to see that wretched display.

The rabbit dangles on a rope secured to a slender tree. I may not have the battle cry of a hunter, but I know a snare when I see one. Sure enough, the rabbit's tracks lead to a cache of bait on the ground. I can't see the hunters' trail, but they'll be back to check the trap in the next day or two.

Dinner ... and *a rescue!*

My heart skips like a smooth stone on the water. Things are looking up for me. Using my knife, I cut the thick noose and toss the limp body in the snow.

Now, how will I let them know where to find me?

They can't see the cliff from here and a snowfall will bury my tracks. I glance around and spy a fallen tree. Dragging it beneath the snare, I add two more logs at its tip to form a great arrow pointing toward my camp.

If it snows, surely they would still see the arrow, and even if they only walked a hundred yards more in that direction, they'll see my fire or smell my supper. I lick my lips, ready for a good feed.

Just the thought of cooked meat stokes my energy. My side

aches, but my mind is on other things, mainly roasted hare. Back at my shelter, I dig a shallow hole in the snow close enough to the rock wall to protect the fire from the wind, but far enough from my boughs to keep my bed from burning. With the thicker sticks pitched like a tiny house in its center, I break the kindling and shove the twigs just inside. I may not remember my name, but at least I seem to recall how to make a fire. And at the moment, that is more important. Perhaps with a bit of warm food in my belly, the rest of my memories will come. I've used my morning's gleanings, all but two last branches I've left leaning on the rock wall behind me—a long thin stick, good for a skewer, and an arm-sized log, my last bit of firewood. I doubt I'll need it. 'Tis twilight now, but even if the trapper doesn't check his line tonight, he'll surely do it tomorrow and not leave it to be scavenged by some wild animal.

Like me. I smile as I squat by the rabbit, knife poised. But my grin fades as I lift it by its hind leg.

How do I skin it? Have I ever done this before?

I place the tip of the knife at its throat, then change my mind and move to the tail.

Is there more than one way to skin a rabbit?

Something tickles at the back of my mind, a joke swimming there below the surface. But I don't fish for the memory. If I remember anything right now, I want it to be how to make my dinner. Something tells me I should slit the underside, up the middle, and peel it off like a little fur glove. Funnily enough, that's exactly what happens. The fur strips away in nearly one piece but, as it comes free, a mess of rabbit innards spill out. They don't seem like anything I want to eat, not when there's fresh rabbit, so I scrape them out and wipe the gory blade in the slush. Soon enough, I've got the small carcass skewered and ready to cook. I flourish it with pride, before propping my meaty flag in the snow.

Imagine the stories they'll tell about me—the great hunter who survived in the wintry woods alone and injured. *How did you manage?* they'll ask. *Sure, 'twas no bother at all,* I'll answer, *not for a woodsman like meself.*

I can't picture the people but I can picture their admiration well enough. It shines from their eyes and warms me at the core. A deep place inside me hungers for that more than any kind of food.

I kneel and strike the flint. Its sparks spray and sputter over the fire pit but neither sticks nor twig will catch. By the fourth attempt, the only flaring is my temper.

Burn, you cursed wood! Or, by God, I swear I'll smash you to smithereens!

I strike the flint, again and again, trembling with the effort and the aggravation of it. But the sparks fade as they rain over the house of cold sticks. On the next strike, my hand slips and I gouge my thumb.

Bloody hell!

Sitting back on my heels, I suck my throbbing thumb and stare off into the woods. This isn't working. I'll have worn through the flint itself before the sticks and twigs catch. I need something to hold the flame longer.

A few leaves, stragglers from autumn, rustle in the wind. I circle the clearing and pick some from the bottom branches. This will work. It has to. Squatting by the cold fire pit, I stuff the brittle leaves beneath the kindling.

Holding my breath, I focus on the flint edge as I strike, willing those precious blue sparks to flicker and flare. One catches, burning a red-rimmed hole in one curled leaf, and then another, devouring them in seconds. I pray it will last long enough for the sticks to catch, but as the leaves' tiny blaze sputters and dies so does my hope. More leaves. I should have used more! Frustrated, I curse and whip the flint at the rock wall. Sparks fly off as it strikes, mocking me with their flares. I drop my head into my arms. I'll never be able to cook that rabbit now, and I was so close, so close to eating a cooked meal, I could cry.

My stomach complains, but a faint crackling behind lifts my head and my heart. For there, in the furrow's nook, the abandoned nest blazes. And I declare to God that I never saw a lovelier sight.

Chapter 6

'Tis dark by the time the hare is cooked, but no matter, for I've a grand roaring fire, not to mention a fine bit of meat sizzling over it. Smelling it roast, seeing its juices drip and hiss, I'm near drowned by my mouth's watering. I've half a mind to pull it off the fire and eat it still rare, but I make myself wait. Bloody torture, but I know 'twill be worth it. And it is.

The scorched meat burns my lips, but I can't stop myself. I don't remember my last meal—it may well have been two days ago—but I'm tearing into this meat like I haven't eaten in months. There's nothing in this world right now but me and it. Or so I think.

It's not until I stop to breathe and lean back, greasy-faced, against the rock wall that I see them. A pair of yellow eyes at the edge of the clearing. Watching me.

Not human, that's for sure. Their glow makes me think

they're not even of this world. They seem to float three feet from the ground. Not blinking. Not moving. Just staring.

Skewer still gripped in my hand, I peer past the fire's glare into the shadows. I can just make out a shaggy, dog-like shape behind those ghostly eyes. 'Tis no ghoul or banshee, but knowing it's a wild wolf doesn't make me feel any better.

For all I've forgotten, I remember enough to build a shelter, skin a rabbit, and make a fire. Maybe someone taught it to me. Maybe 'tis my own instinct. Either way, that same voice is telling me now that this wolf means: danger.

We sit and stare at each other for a while. Neither one making a move.

How long has it been there watching me? What is it waiting for?

The flames are dying down and I edge my free hand over to the last log, unsure if I should use it for the fire or as a club. I glance around the darkened clearing but there is only one pair of eyes. So far. If it's the fire that's keeping the wolf at bay, I'd do better to burn this log than wield it. Truth be told, I'd not be able to fight off one of them, much less a whole pack. I add the wood to the embers but it does nothing to ease the chill up my spine as I watch those yellow eyes.

Is it waiting for me to fall asleep?

I want to yell but my "battle cry" would likely do more harm than good. A screech like that would make it think I'm weak and terrified and no doubt provoke an attack. And so we sit and stare. Size each other up. But after what seems like ages, I can take the eerie gaze no longer. "What do you want?" my voice splits the silence of the winter night and I bolt to my feet, heart racing.

The wolf mimics my movements and rises to all fours. If its tail is wagging, I can't see it. Does a wolf even wag its tail?

I raise the skewer and what's left of the rabbit overhead, waving it frantically as I shout. "Go on! Get out of here!"

The wolf takes a small step forward and a rumble travels its throat, erupting through its black lips.

Wonderful. I've gone and angered it now.

With its next step toward me, I launch the skewer, rabbit and all, like a spear. Maybe it'll pierce its side, slow it down, make it think twice about attacking me. But the rabbit carcass weighs down the tip and the great hunter's launch is more of a little boy's lob, landing just in front of the wolf. He looks down, noses the rabbit skeleton, and looks back at me.

"Whisht! Go!" I yell, hoping the panic in my voice is mistaken for threat. "Go on!"

The wolf places a thick paw on the skewer and pulls the rabbit free, breaking the thick stick like it was mere straw. The crack of it makes my stomach lurch, for I daresay my own bones would snap just as easily between those great jaws. Then, rabbit in its maw, it glances at me one last time before disappearing into the night.

I slump, soggy-legged, against the rock face and slide down it, landing in a heap by the fire. I can't stop shaking. From fear. From shock. From excitement. I don't know if the wolf will be back, or what I'll do if it is. But I know one thing for sure: I can't wait to go home when my rescuers come for me tomorrow. I fought off a wolf, probably a whole pack of them, with my bare hands—oh, what a tale I've got to tell!

Chapter 7

"Wake up, *shognosh*." The voice cuts into my wolf dreams, and I open my eyes, to find myself lying against the rock face, squinting at the person standing before me in the early morning light.

Rescued! My heart swells, but before I can speak to this stranger, who looks no older than me, his black eyes narrow. His clothes are different from mine, deerskin, I think, with fringed and beaded mittens, leather leggings, and boots. From under a gray fur hat, his black hair hangs long, like a girl's, on either side of his face, but the slingshot sticking out of his woven belt and the arrows in the quiver on his back, not to mention the look in his eye, make me think I'd best keep my mouth shut.

"Who are you?" he asks.

I shrug. "I was hoping you'd be able to tell me that."

He tilts his head. "Where are you from?"

"I don't know." I rub my bruised forehead. "I think I had some kind of accident and I don't remember anything."

He glances around at my near-dead fire. "Where is the rabbit?"

I have an answer for this one, but the way he's carrying on makes me think he won't like it. Instead, I stall, trying to wake up enough to think straight.

"Rabbit?" I ask, innocently.

"Yes," he leans forward and grabs my chin with his thick hide mitten. "The one from my trap. Its grease is all over your lying face."

"I ate it," I say, slapping his hand away and rising to meet him. He's no bigger than me. I'm not afraid of him. "*I* found it and *I* ate it."

His dark eyes narrow as his jaw clenches. I wonder if he's going to hit me. Instead, he stoops and picks up the bloodied rabbit skin that lies where I left it, shaking his head at the botched skinning job, no doubt. He shoves the peeled pelt in front of me accusingly. "I'll tell you who you are, scavenger. A wasteful thief who steals from the true hunters."

"You aren't here to rescue me, are you?" I say, though I know his answer well enough.

He sneers at my dismal fire and limp bough bedding before giving me the once-over. "You need saving, but it won't be by me." He turns to leave.

"Who are you?" I call, for as much as I dislike the dark-haired boy, I don't want him to leave. Surely he can help me find my way home. "At least tell me where I am."

He marches to the clearing's edge. "I am Mahingan Wawatie. And you are on my family's hunting grounds." And before I can utter a reply, he vanishes with nothing but his footprints to prove he'd been there at all.

I'm fuming, so I am. It takes me most of the morning to calm down as I stomp around, muttering to myself. "You think I *want* to be stuck in your dumb forest?" I take my anger out on the trees, snapping branches and sticks until the pain in my side stops me from doing any more.

"'My family's hunting grounds.'" I snort. "Who does he think he is, the bloody landlord?" I dump the wood beside my dying fire. Add a few sticks to keep it going a little longer. A part of me wonders if I should have followed him. But surely someone will come for me soon and I can get the hell out of here. "You're not the only trapper," I shout to the thick woods, "and you're not even a good one!"

I toss another branch at the fire and stare up at the trail of smoke. Someone is coming for me. They have to be.

CHAPTER 8

The days drag on and, despite my signal fire, neither my father nor any rescuer appears. Though my side seems to be healing slowly, I'm in no shape to venture too far on my own. Daylight hours are spent gathering firewood, melting snow for drinking water, and following a few animal tracks. I figure if I can't find the animal that makes these trails, maybe they'll at least lead me to what that animal is eating. Sure enough, one spoor leads me to a gooseberry bush where a few forgotten berries still dangle, and another takes me to a cache of acorns. If it's good enough for the animals, 'tis good enough for me. Roasted, the nuts aren't half bad. Mind you, they aren't half enough, either, and my stomach sulks and grumbles the rest of the day.

There's been no sight of Mahingan, but I've seen his tracks, too. Coming back to spy on me. Let him. Sure, what do I care? Yesterday, I followed his footprints through the gorge to a lake about a mile away. A puddle of pink slush by the shore told me he'd had a kill. Fish, by the look of it. I still can't figure out how he got them out with that thick ice capping the lake like a lid on a pot. But if he can do it, I daresay I will. And a bigger fish, at that.

I'm kept busy enough trying to find wood and food in daylight hours, but 'tis the long nights that are getting to me. I've spent them whittling a spear. Tonight, I carved a wolf paw print in the soft leather next to my belt buckle, as a reminder. I'd hate to lose that story. Next to it, I etch another small line. Scratches that tell me I've been here far too long. This one makes seven. A whole week.

Why aren't they coming for me? 'Tis in the dark that doubt whispers loudest. *Maybe they aren't looking for me. Maybe they don't want me back.*

Though my injuries are getting better, my mind is in a fog. I pocket the knife and bang my head with my fist, trying to jar the memories loose. If only I could remember something ... *something* about how I got here, about where I'm from. I wouldn't need to wait for some blasted rescue party. If I knew where I was or who I was, sure, I could get up and walk out of here myself. But my memories lie at the bottom of my mind, like the trout in the frozen lake, and, try as I might—and I've tried all these long, dark hours—I can think of no way to fish them out.

The wolf has come the past three nights. It usually sits not a hundred yards away, just watching. I wonder what it's waiting for. Maybe it's looking at me, wondering the very same thing. A few nights ago, heart hammering in my chest, I just started talking to it. Partly out of nerves. I thought that the sound of my voice might keep it at bay and, strangely enough, it did. After my rambling yarn about an amazing and courageous boy who survives a great adventure in the wild, the wolf simply stood and disappeared into the silent woods. It has come the next night and the next, each time sitting a bit closer and closer. I tell myself it's coming to hear my stories so that I don't have to think about the truth of it. 'Tis easier to handle its eerie gaze when I think 'tis my tales and not my tail that it's hungering after.

But there is no sign of it tonight and that's all the more unsettling. As much as those yellow eyes unnerve me, at least they tell me where it is. Better the devil you see than the one you don't. I put my belt on and scan the black strip of the woods' silhouette, blind to whatever hides in its depths. Has the wolf gone to rally the pack? It's seen me grow weaker with hunger these past few days. Easy prey. Maybe tonight is the night. I shiver and huddle into my bed of boughs, trying not to think about the growling in my empty stomach or what might be growling in the woods.

CHAPTER 9

Hours later, in the heavy darkness, an unfamiliar sound behind me rips me from sleep. In an instant, I'm awake, eyes wide, staring through the black at the rock wall before me.

There it is again.

Even over my blood drumming, I hear the faint squeak and crunch of feet upon snow. What my eyes can't tell me, my gut already knows.

'Tis the wolf. Coming for me.

It's done watching. Tonight the wolf is making its move. And so must I. My mind scurries in a panic, like a mouse in a box, twitching from one dead end to another. *Knife?* Buried in the pocket beneath me. I couldn't get it out in time. *Spear?* Left on the other side of the fire. Even if I could roll and grab it before the wolf lunges, what good would it do? The image of the wolf snapping my rabbit skewer flashes before me—

surely, it would do the same with my spear. Or my bones. Run? *Where?* I'm trapped between wolf and wall.

The slow steps creak to a stop just behind me on the other side of the dying fire. I don't have to hear its wet panting to know it's there. Can't I feel the weight of its yellow stare? Its very presence crushes me. I can't breathe.

"*R-r-r- r,*" a low noise rolls up its throat and over its teeth on hot breath. "*R-r-r-ruff.*"

There's nothing to do but face it. I slowly roll to my back, turn my head to where it stands in the embers' eerie glow. The sight of the creature looming on slender legs both terrifies and amazes me. Be it fear or awe, and probably both, I still can't take a breath. There is nothing but the wolf and my heart beating in my head.

Its broad chest of black-tipped, creamy fur rises and falls as each pant passes through its bloodstained muzzle. But it isn't the fresh blood that holds my stare, nor the deadly fangs behind those black lips. 'Tis the eyes. Framed beneath their dark brows, they seem almost human. More than human, truth be told. For they're wise. Ageless. Not yellow, but gold, fresh from the blacksmith's forge, flecked with amber and flickering firelight. And when their black centers find mine, I feel seen. Known.

Ears pricked, the wolf arches one brow and tilts its head ever so slightly. It seems as intrigued by me, though I can't imagine what's interesting about a boy in a bed of boughs, and a scrawny boy, at that. Neither of us moves for a long time. Or so it seems. Then the wolf lowers its head and starts to step forward.

Scrambling back, I hit the wall. There's nowhere for me to go, now. I want to scream, but no sound comes. Nosing something forward, the wolf stops right in front of me, and all I can think is, *Lord in heaven, he's breathtaking,* as I reach up to touch its creamy coat, just once. The wolf's bloodied muzzle turns to my hand and I freeze midair, but somehow, somewhere, I know he won't hurt me.

His twitching black nose reaches for my fingertips, sniffs, and, satisfied, lowers to nudge a small carcass up onto my lap. A pheasant, or at least I think it was. 'Tis half devoured and a right bloody mess, yet there's still good eating on what's left.

The wolf takes a step back, looks at the bird and then at me.

"Thank you," I whisper. My voice cracks the silence, breaking the spell. The wolf turns, lunges back to the wood, then stops at the clearing's edge for one last look with those golden eyes, before melting into the shadows.

CHAPTER 10

I thought I'd dreamt the wolf's visit, but the half-eaten pheasant I'd cooked and finished for breakfast the next morning was real enough. The wolf could have attacked me in my sleep, it could have eaten me ... and I touched it—petted it, no less! Wait until I tell them—

Them. Despite my fire's signal, there's been no sign of them, whoever they are. No scent of home on the cold air. No sounds but winter's silence. Touching the wolf emboldened me—as though some of its spirit had seeped from fur to fingers. Enough waiting. 'Tis high time I take matters into my own hands. My side's near healed and, though my head still aches fierce from time to time, I can handle a trek. I think. How far can it be? Not very—if I am walking in the right direction. Mind you, figuring out exactly which direction is the problem.

And so I walk. Each day I choose a direction and venture

a bit further into the woods, hoping I'll stumble upon a farm fence or country road that might lead me back to what I can't recall. I've seen glimpses of them in my dreaming. But so far, all I find in my waking is more wilderness.

After another afternoon of finding nothing but bare trunks and thick evergreen, I am losing hope. My home might well be a stone's throw away from where I stand and I'll not see it. *Like a needle in a haystack*, some familiar voice echoes in my brain. I know the saying but not the sayer, and that only frustrates me all the more.

"Trees, trees, and more bloody trees!" I yell, startling a hawk from the oak's top branches. "Tell me, then," I shout at it. "Tell me what you see." For if my home is nearby, surely that bird has spied it. But it doesn't answer. After the wolf encounter, half of me expects the hawk to settle on my shoulder and whisper in my ear—*'tis only down the way, lad. You're nearly there.*

Nearly mad, the other half thinks.

"Bad enough I can't remember a thing," I mutter. "Now, I'm cursing trees and berating birds—not to mention talking to myself." I sigh, still wishing I could see what that bird sees. "And why can't I?"

I don't remember climbing trees, but I surely have, for, with little thought and even less effort, I scurry up the oak.

Moving limb to limb like a right squirrel, I climb until the slender branches near the top bend beneath my weight. Without the shelter of the forest, the biting wind skips along the treetops, stopping to gnaw at my cheeks. It stings my eyes and makes them water, but I rub them on my mitten and scan the horizon, twice to be sure. There has to be some clue, a sign, *something* to give me a sense of which way leads home, but all I see is a thawing river, cutting through miles upon miles of rolling forest. A gray sea of wood. And me adrift in the middle of it.

The climb down is slow going, but what's the rush? *Is there any point in trekking further? Is there any point in waiting to be found? Is there any point at all?*

I just want to sit down and cry. For a moment, I think I will. But if someone *is* looking for me, the last thing I'd want is for them to come upon me blubbering like a right fool.

And if they're not looking for me?

Well, I wipe my runny nose on the back of my mitten, *if they're not looking, well then, crying's no help, neither.*

My stomach rumbles, reminding me of how long it's been since it had that pheasant. Knowing which way to go is no use if I don't have food, if I don't keep up my strength. Picking up my spear, I follow the gorge, a trail I know will take me to the lake. To fish. Now all I have to do is figure out how to catch one.

CHAPTER 11

Trudging through the snow warms me up, but I'm careful not to overheat. Sweating only makes me that much colder once I stop moving. I'd learned that the hard way while gathering wood a few days ago.

With every step, the snow rises and falls, rises and falls, like whitecaps spilling off a ship's prow. *And me the figurehead.* I smile at the thought. For I'm nothing like the mythical women carved on ships' prows, with their wild hair and full bosoms. Sure, I don't even look like the bearded monk carved on the front of my ship.

I stop. *My ship.*

His wooden face is as clear to me as the trees before me, hair carved as though caught in the sea wind as he gazes out at the wide horizon. I remember studying his chiseled profile before I boarded, desperately trusting he would bring me to that distant place he'd set his sights upon. *Don't look back. Don't look back.*

And yet now, I can't. I close my eyes, try to see more than his face. *What is this ship? Who is with me? Where are we going?* But I see nothing. The memories are buried deep, like summer grass, waiting for the thaw. And I can do nothing but stare at wide, blank white and wait.

"Dunbrody," I whisper the word, unsure if it is his name or mine. Or perhaps the place I left. A sharp wind swirls the snow around me, bringing me back to the woods. "Dunbrody," I repeat. I know this name, I do, and I don't want to let it go for fear I'll lose it forever. Setting down my spear, I pull out my knife and take off my belt. The brown leather is worn, but smooth enough for the task at hand. Slipping off my mittens, I rest the belt on a fallen tree and beside the wolf print and days' tally, begin to carve the tired leather. *D* ... *U* ... *N* ... my fingers sting from the cold and I stop to rub them, blow some heat into their icy cup. I know enough to take my time with the carving. A slip of the knife would prove costly. *B* ... *R* ... *O* ... *D* ... *Y*. Finally, I finish. The letters along the middle of the strap are small and crooked, but legible. Permanent. Satisfied, I pocket the knife, rub my reddened hands, don mittens and belt, and continue deeper into the world of white.

The gorge trail leads me to the lake, a great slab of ice, rimmed by barren sticks and stalks. Traveling the shoreline, I search for the best fishing site, but even with the recent thaw and bit of water lapping the shore, the ice is still too thick. No fish are in the shallows. *Where then?* I wonder. For surely, Mahingan has found some. *Deeper? But how did he get them?*

My eyes drift over the sheet of white, stopping on a darker patch about a hundred yards offshore. It hits me then. *If the lake is frozen, you just walk on it to deeper waters. Simple.* I fairly glow with pride, and rightly so. For there's none can outsmart me. Not even that Mahingan. "My family hunting grounds," I sneer as I gingerly step onto the ice, but 'tis solid enough. "Whose forest is it now, boyo?"

CHAPTER 12

Snippets of a story come to mind—a man, Peter, I think, tries to walk on water but sinks because he doesn't believe. I can scarce believe it myself. This is solid ice, I tell myself, yet with every gust of wind, every time I look back at the shore disappearing behind me and imagine the lake deepening beneath me, panic ripples in my gut. This is madness!

A loud crack echoes from behind. I turn, half expecting to see Mahingan there, chopping firewood, or standing, slingshot cocked, aiming his next shot at me, but the shore is empty. I curse myself for being so jumpy, blame it on the lake. The sooner the better I'm off this thing. I spy the hole. It's about a foot across, if that. *So, that's how he does it.* The discovery delights me, so it does. Without the ice lid to stop me, I know now I can catch as many fish as I can eat. But the delight doesn't last long, for as I squat to peer into the circle of black water, I realize this hole is too dark, too small. Even if there is a fish in there, I'll not see it.

A small snowball hits my cheek like an ice fist. I shake my head to make the ringing stop, only to hear him shouting, "... you *pwanawito ... ininigoban!* "

Mahingan. I should have known. He's pacing back and forth, arms flailing as he yells from the shoreline, his glare colder than the ice melting down my neck. I have no idea what he's saying, and, by the sound of it, that's probably just as well. I wipe my stinging face and, standing, turn to the shore as I rest the butt of my spear on the ice. He doesn't scare me. "You don't own this lake!" I shout back. "Keep your bloody hole, I'll dig my—"

A thunderous *crack* rings out like a shot. For a second, I think it is a gun—only it came from beneath my feet.

The ice!

The terror on Mahingan's face mirrors my own. But before I can move a muscle, before I can take another breath, the ice beneath my feet splinters and explodes, plunging me into the frigid lake, and I'm swallowed in biting cold. Stunned, I sink into numbness for a few long seconds—

No!

Kicking hard, I break the water's surface. Coughing. Gasping for air. I claw at the ice, desperate for a hold. 'Tis as though time itself has slowed, sodden, frigid, and heavy. Twice, I get a grip and thrust with my legs. I no sooner mount the ice's edge when it shatters beneath me and I'm submerged once again. The cold crushes me, squeezes my lungs, squashes my brain. I can't last much longer. I haven't the strength. 'Tis as though some creature wants to pull me to the depths. Swallow me in darkness. Giving in, I sink one last time.

Already, my soul has left my hands and feet, for I feel them no longer. Light ripples above, only inches away, but even that seems so far.

Too far.

CHAPTER 13

"Da?" I shiver.

Someone raises my head, presses a cup to my lips. The hot, sweet tea radiates like an ember rolling down my chest as I swallow. It feels good. Like the glow of hearth light from a window at the end of a long, dark road. The promise of home.

I wonder if I am there now. My memory strains with my eyes as they focus on the sapling framework crisscrossing overhead, the smoke drifting through the hole into the black sky. The scent of evergreen fills my head. Helps it clear. No, this isn't home. For as surely as I don't know where I am, I do know I've never been here before.

I want to get up, get answers, but the shadow beside me lowers my head and I haven't the strength to lift it. Once again, I feel myself going down. The swallowing darkness. The sense that something is dragging me under. Only this time, it's warm and welcoming and I sink into it wholeheartedly.

"You snore like a snuffling skunk."

Something pokes my shoulder, waking me from my deepest sleep in ages. I know I slept like the dead, for I can't for the life of me recall who I am or where I am, but even as my mind comes to—neither are answered. The only thing I do know is the lad before me, the one poking me with that bloody stick.

"Mahingan," I mutter, rubbing my head, annoyed that the one thing I can recall is the person I least want to. "Where am I?"

I look around the small dwelling. 'Tis as though we are under a great cone of bark. The floor, a circle twelve feet across, is carpeted in fresh evergreen boughs. A hide, much like the one covering me, hangs over what must be the door. Dangling from a long rope, a pot simmers over the fire in the middle. Mahingan pokes at the embers. There's no one here but him and me. I feel for my knife, surprised to discover that under this fur blanket, I'm as naked as the day I was born. "Where's my knife," I blurt, "and my clothes?"

Mahingan jabs at the burning log with his poking stick. "You call that a knife?"

"My father gave it to me," I say. "I want it back."

He draws a large knife from the sheath by the fire. "This is my father's knife. One worthy of a great son." He flourishes its shining blade at me. I cringe, but only because I'm naked, unarmed, and vulnerable. He doesn't scare me. Not really. If I had my knife or my spear, or even a pair of breeches, I'd take him.

"Judging by how you skinned *my* rabbit," he looks at me, "a good knife would just be wasted on you."

That's it. Pants or not, he's getting it. I fling the mound of hides and lunge for him. Be it my ferocity or, more likely, the sight of my naked body, winter white and mottled with yellow-green bruises, leaping for him, I catch him by surprise and gain the advantage. But it doesn't last long. For a small lad, he's fair strong. Next thing I know, I'm on my back and he is straddling across my chest, knife at my throat.

"I'll show you how it's done." A grin seeps across his dark face. "Let's skin a skunk."

CHAPTER 14

"Mahingan!" The word is hard and sharp, striking its target dead center. The man's voice is surprisingly powerful, given his lean frame. He says something to Mahingan in a language I don't understand, but his tone is clear enough. Mahingan relents, shifting his weight off me.

If the old man entering through the door is surprised to see a white, buck-naked boy wrestling at his fireside, he doesn't show it. Instead, he opens his hand and waits for Mahingan to lay the great knife in his palm. I wonder if the old man will strap him for that. Pulling a knife on a guest, and a sickly guest at that. But the old man seems more upset about the fact that Mahingan touched the knife than by what the boy was doing with it.

Sheathing the blade once more, he reverently returns Mahingan's father's knife by the fire.

Mahingan, flustered, gestures at me as though 'tis my fault he attacked me with a knife. "*Mishomis,* he—"

The old man raises his hand, cutting Mahingan short. He's built like Mahingan, lean and wiry, with the same dark eyes, same nose and cheekbones whittled to sharp points. They must be related. His father? No, too old. Grandfather, then. Still, for a small man, there's a certain power about him. His long hair may be white and his skin weathered, but his presence alone leads me to think that underneath the icy exterior, the current runs strong and deep.

He grasps my clothes, draped over sticks on the other side of the fire. I hadn't even noticed them there, but the sight of them reminds me I'm naked. I reach for them but, once again, the old man holds up his hand. "Patience." His English is as good as Mahingan's, but his accent is richer, bolder, like a well-steeped tea. He makes no move to give me the clothes, though they look dry enough. Still, I'm a good bit shaky and my head aches. I know I'm too weak to leave just yet, so I sit down and wrap myself in one of the hides as Mahingan scowls. Besides, whatever's simmering smells inviting, even if Mahingan's face is not.

I wait for his grandfather to ask me questions. Surely, he's wondering where I came from or what my name is, at least. But he doesn't speak. Slowly, he fills a bowl with hot liquid from the pot of boiling bones. He hands it to me and another to Mahingan, before settling fireside with his own. My stomach rumbles as the steam wafts into my face. As good as it smells, and as hungry as I am, 'tis answers I most want—only no one's offering any. The three of us slurp in silence until I can take it no longer.

"Do you know me?" I blurt. "I mean, do you know who I am? Where I came from?" Even as I say it, each question sounds more ridiculous.

The old man doesn't look up from his steaming bowl. I wonder if he's slightly deaf. I speak a bit louder.

"It's just I think ... I think I'm lost ..." My voice cracks on the last word and my eyes burn. It must be the steam or maybe the smoke from the fire.

Mahingan snorts. The man cocks his white eyebrow, and his dark gaze smothers any further sounds from the boy.

So not deaf, not by a long shot. Still, the old man's silence tells me he can't help me. He doesn't know the answers.

"Crane," he says, between sips, his full attention on his bowl.

"That's my family name?" I ask.

"By the river, he stands on one leg. For hours he does not move. But when a fish swims by—splash!" The man's arm snaps out and back before closing in a tight fist. "He grabs it."

Mahingan simply nods, satisfied with the man's strange words, and returns to his soup. But the random animal story only frustrates me. What the blazes is he talking about? Is he mad?

"Do you know me or not," I blurt, respectfully adding "... sir." For crazy or not, the man is my elder.

"I know you." He sets down his bowl. Wipes his chin. Takes his time.

I'm near bursting with impatience. "What's my name, then?"

He just stares at the fire.

"My family—who are they?"

Again, he simply waits. Picks his teeth.

"You don't know." I yell. "You don't know anything!"

Mahingan jumps to his feet and lunges for me, but his grandfather's touch holds him back, settles him down.

"*Mishomis*," Mahingan pleads, "he cannot talk to you that way."

The old man turns his dark eyes on me for a second and 'tis as though he's looking into my very soul. "I know you." He looks back at the fire. "The question is, do you know you? What is your name?"

I know it. Feel it rippling round the back of my mind.

"Tell me about your family," he says.

I want to name them. The knowing swims just beneath the surface. I can almost reach it. "I've dreamt about them," I say, ashamed that's all I've got.

The corners of his eyes wrinkle slightly. "Good. That is good."

"My father ... and my sister," I continue, recalling the knife dream. "I was younger. He was teaching me how to whittle, and I cut myself." I finger the faint scar on my hand.

"Scars can teach us many things," the man says. The fire pops and crackles in the silence.

"That's all." I shrug. "Why can't I remember any more than that? I could leave now, if only I knew where home was."

"Patience," the old man repeats. "The answers will surface."

"But when?"

He waits so long to answer, I think he's not going to. "You wait as long as it takes," his voice speaks, breaking the silence. "Be still, watchful. And when it is time, act."

"Like the crane," I say, as a few pieces of this puzzling man fit together.

He nods and returns to his soup.

CHAPTER 15

"Today, you will go with Mahingan," Grandfather Wawatie says.

The muscles on Mahingan's jaw tighten. He's biting his words, so he is. He looks me over, his dislike as cold and clear as the blue sky. He tries to reason with his grandfather. "He probably wants to get going, him. Find his family, I mean."

I do, of course. Only, I've still no idea which way leads home. I glance at the thick forest on either side of me. I had hoped Mahingan's grandfather might give me some answers. But all he's given me are riddles. Stories. Even the most direct questions got no results. "Where are we?" I'd asked over our breakfast.

"We are here," he'd finally answered and chuckled with Mahingan as though I'd asked a most ridiculous thing.

Outside their small, bark-covered shelter, the old man

slips an empty bag across his back and secures his snow-shoes—great netted hoops—beneath each foot. "You are an extra pair of eyes and hands," the grandfather tells me. He ties their dog to the toboggan. "We will check the nets along Flat Rock. You two check the beaver lodge." He eyes the bright sky. "Maybe the snow will hold off." With that, he turns and disappears into the field of gray trunks and white-capped firs.

"You don't have to take me," I offer. For I've no desire to spend the afternoon with Mahingan, either. "I can stay here."

"And steal our food," Mahingan snaps. "You eat with us—you work with us."

I open my mouth to protest, but he does have a point. After all, I did take his rabbit. He'll not let me forget that. And they've fed me a few meals. I'll stay the day. Hunt with him. Pay my debt. And maybe later get some kind of information from the old man. Even if he doesn't know me, surely he knows where the nearest town lies. I watch where the man has disappeared into the forest and it occurs to me that maybe they're lost, too. After all, there's only the pair of them in the middle of this wide wood. Maybe they've no idea where we are, either.

"Carry this," Mahingan orders, interrupting my thoughts. He tosses me what looks like a paddle. I catch the long wooden handle and notice it ends in a scoop. A shovel of sorts.

"And you can pull the toboggan, too." He hesitates. "Unless you're too weak from your last *hunting* trip."

I'm not fully recovered, but I'll not tell him that. "Fine," I say, lowering the toboggan from where it rests against a birch tree. I slip the rope over my shoulders and settle it across my chest. "But I may need help pulling it when it's loaded up with all my game."

I don't know what I'm talking about. Sure, haven't I been in the woods over a week now and all I've found is Mahingan's rabbit. Still, he doesn't know that.

"Well, when I kill my bear, it will be so big, we will need two toboggans to bring it home," he brags, so full of himself. "Grandfather will surely give me my father's knife then."

I wonder why his father isn't using his own knife, but, more than that, I wonder what else might be lurking in those trees. I glance at him. "There are bears here?"

Mahingan snorts as he walks ahead, easily cutting a trail with his snowshoes.

I'm not afraid—I mean, I've heard about bears, great giant beasts. I didn't mean to sound so nervous. 'Tis just a question, is all.

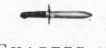

CHAPTER 16

I'm panting like a plough horse as I trudge through the heavy snow, dragging this blasted toboggan behind while Mahingan scurries along on his snowshoes. For such foolish-looking contraptions, I admit they do seem to make walking easier. Mahingan barely sinks in the snow at all, while I'm here up to my knees, heaving great foggy breaths as I forge ahead, inch by inch. He's taking me through the deepest drifts on purpose, I swear he is.

After what seems like hours, we arrive at a clearing in the wood with two hillocks in the center of a frozen river. The larger one is near double the size of the smaller one farther downstream. Mahingan takes off his snowshoes and, picking up his ax, strikes the ice near the smaller mound's edge.

With a few good chops, he soon hits water and chips at the hole until it's about a foot and a half wide. He climbs onto the mound and swings his ax at the branches between his feet.

"What are you doing?" I have to ask, as frigid water starts to gush from the holes. The thatch is sure to collapse.

"Trenching the dam," he says, barely winded from all his chopping. "Cut a hole here and the water level inside the lodge lowers."

"So?"

"So the beaver will come out to fix the dam—and then I'll catch him."

I realize then that the larger stick-covered hump is the beaver's home. If this huge pile of muck and twig is its nest, I can only imagine what size of creature lives in it.

"Well?" he says, looking at me expectantly.

"Well, what?" I shiver just looking at that gushing ice water. There's no way I'm going anywhere near it.

"Bang the lodge," says he, like I've any idea what he means. He rolls his eyes and gestures at the main lodge. "Climb up there and hit the lodge with the shovel. Scare it out."

"How do you know it's even in there?" I ask, stalling, for there's no sense in me risking a climb over a river for naught. He nods at a small opening on the top of the lodge where slight steam escapes like a wee chimney. Something is living in there.

Steeling myself, I gingerly step on to the lodge. A few

skinny twigs snap under my weight. "Will this hold me?" I stomp my boot. The thatch underneath seems sound enough. Making my way to the lodge's midpoint, I whack it with my shovel.

What if the sticks collapse?

What if I fall in the river?

Or worse yet, fall through the nest?

A vision of me swarmed by a hive of angered beavers freezes me for a second. "What do beavers eat?" I ask, trying to sound like I'm just making conversation.

"Yellow-headed boys who ask too many questions," Mahingan answers.

CHAPTER 17

I'm starting to think this is just some elaborate trap Mahingan is setting to land me in the river again. I glance at the beaver lodge beneath my feet, at the thick, silent woods around us. No one to hear me scream. I could die out here and no one would be any the wiser.

But it seems Mahingan has already forgotten about me as he turns and lies flat on his stomach by the hole in the ice. I grip the shovel tighter and beat the lodge with all my might. The sooner it's out, the sooner I can get back on land.

Taking off his mittens and pushing up his sleeves, Mahingan thrusts both arms deep into the frigid water. He is mad, that one. But just as I'm about to ask what in God's name he's doing, he lets out a yelp and starts thrashing about.

The beaver! It's got him!

Shovel in hand, I clamber over the lodge back to the shore,

sure Mahingan will be dragged through that ice hole any second. But as I reach him, I realize 'tis Mahingan who's doing the dragging. With reddened arms, he pulls the beaver's limp body out of the water and triumphantly raises its slick, steaming carcass overhead. I've never seen anything like it. Part fish, part fur, mostly fang. I swear, 'tis as big as a fair-sized dog with a flat tail like a paddle. Glossy, brown fur covers its body, and from its front paws hang wee gloved hands while the back ones dangle, webbed and razor sharp. Two great, orangey teeth curve over its chin like scythe blades and I wonder if they can cut through bone as easily as wood. I want to touch it. Poke it with a stick. But I can do nothing but stare in awe. Mahingan's chest puffs up like a bellows. Still, I have to give him credit, he did catch it. Barehanded. With my help, of course.

"Did you choke it?" I ask.

"Drowned it," he brags. "My father taught me that they hold their breath long, but not forever—"

With a shriek, the beaver gasps back to life and I jump. Apparently, it can hold its breath longer than Mahingan thought. Thrashing in Mahingan's grip, the beaver whips its body side to side, whacking its heavy tail against Mahingan as it scrabbles with its claws. One snags Mahingan's thigh and as he flinches, the beaver sinks its front teeth deep into his bare forearm. Mahingan screams and drops his catch.

I'm not sure how hurt he is, but my mind is on the beaver running for the ice hole. Raising the shovel I swing it hard and catch the animal on the back, once, twice, three times. Bleeding and stunned, it drops.

"The ax!" Mahingan gasps. I grab it and stand over the beaver, now lying in the snow a foot from its freedom. From its home. I hesitate. *What am I doing?* I've no idea how to kill it, or even if I want to. *Do I cleave it in two? Chop off its head?* The ax weighs heavy in my hand, for I can bring myself to do neither. Whimpering, the beaver starts to come to.

"Do it!" Mahingan yells. He's clutching his arm, limping toward me. "Finish it!"

But I can't.

Snatching the ax with his good hand, Mahingan deals the death blow in one quick motion, bringing down the blunt end on the animal's head, stopping its heart. Forever.

"Well," I clear my throat, trying to hide the sick feeling that's come over me. "We hunters sure showed that beaver, didn't—"

Mahingan's glare is biting cold and my words dissolve. Despite the blood staining his thigh and dripping from his forearm, he leans over the beaver and whispers something. A prayer, I think. And I realize then that he felt it, too. The awe. The guilt. And yet, he did what had to be done.

"You are no hunter," he says, swaying as he rises to his feet.

"A true hunter respects its prey. Kills swiftly, with gratitude."
He looks me over. "What are you? Cruel or just a coward?"

I glance at the bloodied beaver carcass, my eyes burning, and look away, ashamed of both what I couldn't do and of what we did.

CHAPTER 18

Blood from Mahingan's wounds drip into the snow where he kneels. The cuts are deep, especially the one on his arm. Even after he binds it with moss and a strip of hide from his pack, it doesn't take long to bleed through his sleeve. He pushes himself up, only to stagger again after a few steps. He'll not make it home, not like that. But he won't listen to me. Won't let me pull him on the toboggan.

After a half-hour of stumbling, he falls again—only this time he doesn't rise. I run up and kneel by him, roll him over on his back. "Mahingan ... Mahingan, can you hear me?"

His eyes roll in his head and before they focus on me, he's already trying to stand. Grabbing his other arm, I shift him onto the toboggan behind me, settling him next to the beaver.

"Lay down," I say. "I'll pull both your carcasses home."

"I don't need your help." He tries to stand but can't. Still, he won't give up.

"Right, then," I stand over him arms folded, "keep pushing yourself until you pass out. Night's closing in and I've no idea where your camp is."

I can tell that needing my help is more painful than any injury. Gritting his teeth, he finally leans forward and loosens the ties over his boots. "Here ... take my snowshoes."

I step onto the webbing between the hooped wood frame and tie the thick, leather strings around my boots. With these, we'll be home in no time. But, as I step forward, the frames clatter off one another and I end up face first in the snow. Mahingan snorts on the sled behind, but his laughter is cut short by his pain. Still, it's enough to make me even more committed to doing this right. How hard can it be? He made it look so easy. I concentrate on one foot, step gingerly on the snow, but, as I move forward, I forget about clearing the other foot and, once again, end up blowing snow plugs out my nose.

"Widen your stance," he says from his seat.

"Widen your stance," I mutter. "I'll widen your stance for you." I want to take these blasted snowshoes and hit him over the head. He thinks he's so perfect.

I go slower this time, find a rhythm, and swing my feet around to clear each shoe before stepping down. I stagger a few times, but I've got the hang of it. Leaning forward, I push against the toboggan rope. The sled's load is tripled now with Mahingan on it. For a slip of a thing, he's as heavy as a load of lumber.

I'm surely steaming after a good hour of trudging and pulling. I wonder how much farther it is to camp. "Are we almost there?" I ask, breathless, but there's no answer. Stopping, I glance back to find Mahingan unconscious. I call his name and he mumbles in reply.

How long has he been out? I look back at our tracks in the snow. *How far have I gone off course?*

Again, it seems I have nothing but questions. But one thing is sure. Night is seeping in. Given the sliver of moon, I know 'twill be dark soon. Very dark.

Something flashes among the trees just ahead and turns. I'd know those golden eyes anywhere. It blinks and stops a few paces farther to look back. It wants me to follow. And so I do. Though I lose sight of the wolf among the trees a few times, 'tis easy enough to track him. Even in the twilight, dark paw prints dimple the bluish snow. I can follow him, but I wonder where he's leading.

Two boys and a beaver to boot, delivered right to the den's door—his hungry pack would love that, now, wouldn't they?

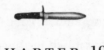

CHAPTER 19

I follow the wolf's trail over a small hill. I'm growing weary now—and wary. It probably wasn't wise to use all my energy to follow a wild animal rather than build a lean-to. I'm sweating and I know how quickly I'll chill, once I stop moving. We have to find shelter. A rock or bluff, anything to get us through the night. As I crest the hill, a shiver ripples up my neck. Not from cold, but from recognition. I know this place, this clearing. I've been here before. The wolf is nowhere to be seen.

Following my instincts, I veer to the left by a great boulder. Just ahead there's a fallen log. I see it clear as day in my mind's eye, and then, there it is. My heart races. *I know this place!*

I start to run and trip over the blasted snowshoes, but it doesn't matter. None of it does. With renewed strength, I drag that heavy load up over the ridge, sure that a dwelling is nestled just on the other side.

And ... there it is. The shanty.

Enormous logs stacked seven high form the wide walls, interlacing at the corners like fingers in prayer. Above them squats a snow-capped roof with a wide chimney peeking through. The great mound reminds me of the beaver lodge.

Have I been here before?

Maybe, but the darkened doorway and dead cold chimney assure me that no one lives here now. I drag the sled to the entrance and try to rouse Mahingan.

"I don't need your help ..." he mutters as I ease him up off the sled. Ignoring his protests, I open the door and lay him on the bunk to the right. I know this place like the back of my hand, I swear I do. The rough-hewn floorboards, the barrels stacked in the corner, the grindstone, even the hodgepodge of pots and kettles left along the ten-foot timbers that frame the great sand-filled fire pit—all of it looks familiar. The room itself is thirty by forty, most of it bunk beds. They line the side and back walls. Whatever family lives here is surely large. The place reeks of smoke, musty woolens, and the tang of old sweat. Just the smell of it gives me a flash of knowing. Bars of a reel. Weathered men laughing round the fire. I can almost snatch the memory, 'tis so near the surface.

Mahingan moans. Remembering will have to wait.

I check his thigh through the tear in his leggings. 'Tisn't too bad. The long scrape seems shallow and is already crusted over with blackened scab. But the gash in his arm is deep. The moss he'd put on it seems to have helped a bit. If nothing else, the cold has slowed the bleeding, but his hands are like ice and his lips tinged with blue around his chattering teeth.

Blanket ... where would I find a blanket?

Sure enough, I spy one on the bunk above him, but even its wool is chilled. We need a fire. Now.

Firewood ... I bet there's some stacked outside.

Along the side of the shanty, I find a mound of it under the new fallen snow. I stop for a moment, wonder how I knew it would be there, but then chide myself. For where else would people store wood? Taking an armload of logs, I return to the shanty and pile some in the fire pit. My hand instinctively reaches for the leather pouch nailed to the post. I know before I open it there'll be a flint inside. Minutes later, I'm warming my hands over a crackling blaze.

Melting a bit of snow in one of the black pots by the fire pit, I give Mahingan a drink before quenching my own thirst. His color seems better, his breathing deep and sound. I don't know what to do for his arm—'tisn't gushing, but a long slow leak can be just as deadly. I wish his grandfather were here. He'd know what to do.

Throwing another log on the fire, I stare at the flames as my eyes grow heavy. Orange light flickers, throwing shadows on bunks lining the walls.

Who lived here? Where are they now?

I want to stay awake, to remember. I knew where to find the blanket and wood, common sense, really ... but the flint? How did I know about that pouch? I yawn. The day's adventure and long trek has worn me out. In any case, it seems my memory is as empty as the beds. Stretching out in a lower bunk, I snuggle under my blanket and let my eyes drift shut.

Maybe Mahingan's grandfather is right. I just need to be patient. I'll leave all those unanswered questions, hang them like wet socks before the fire, and, free of their cold itch, if only for a little while, settle in for the night.

CHAPTER 20

"This place?!"

I bolt awake, thunking my head on the bunk timbers above me. It takes a moment or two for my mind to clear, but 'tisn't long to realize it's Mahingan ranting. I guess he's feeling better.

He flings the blanket off and jumps out of his bunk like it's on fire. "Why did you bring me here?"

"You're welcome," I say, rubbing my temple as I sit and let my legs dangle over the bunk's edge, "for saving your life."

"I didn't need saving."

"So it's in the snow I should've left you, then?"

He glares at me and stomps out the door, returning moments later with his snowshoes, which he awkwardly ties, given his injured arm. He stands and looks around the room in disgust. "Why didn't you take me to my home instead of ... *here.*"

I don't know what his problem is. "What's wrong with it? Beds. Blankets. A fire. It's got thick log walls ... not a few scraps of bark. And the floors are solid planks, not sprigs and branches." I wasn't planning on slagging his home but, still, I'm only saying the truth of it.

He looks like he wants to choke me with his bare hands. For a moment, I think he might. My heart is pounding. I still don't know what we're arguing about. But if he comes at me, I'll kick him in his wounded thigh, bite him myself, so I will.

He turns and heads outside. Stopping to pick up the toboggan rope, he faces me once more, his voice as hard and cold as the beaver carcass. "You come here," he says, his jaw tight, "you ignorant hunters. You know nothing about the ways of the forest."

The beaver? Is that what this is about? He's not going to let me forget that, is he?

"You don't belong here," he continues. "Go back to where you came from before you destroy it all."

The anger shoved upon me makes me push back. "I *want* to go back to where I came from, you *gobshite!* You think I like wandering in the woods? You think I want to be lost?"

"You *kopadizi shognosh!*" He spits the words at me. "You don't even know where you are or what you have done."

"Where am I? What have I done?" I demand. "Tell me! For the love of God, please tell me!" If he knows something, anything about me, I'm desperate to find out. "You don't know," I say, trying a different tack. "You don't know a thing about me."

"I know all about you." He looks me over. "You come here. Work for them. You steal from the land of my ancestors. Destroy dens and nests. You don't care about the ways of the forest. About the animals. You don't care about the *Anish-naabeg*. Yes, I know all about you."

I'm stunned. Part of me wonders what the hell he's talking about. I haven't done those things. Have I?

"Just ... just show me how to get home." I say. "I won't ever come back, I promise—"

His eyes flare. *"Promise?"* He spits on the ground between us. "Your empty words mean nothing to me."

"Fine," I say. "Just tell me which way civilization is. I'll find it on my own."

He laughs and turns. "I don't know what you call civilization, *shognosh*, but my home, my people, are this way."

And with that, he walks off into the woods.

CHAPTER 21

Good riddance. That Mahingan, he's crazy, I swear. Talking nonsense. So he hates shanties—he didn't need to take it out on me. I throw another log on the fire and poke it awake.

What's his problem, anyway? This place is brilliant, so warm and sturdy. Even if it isn't quite as cozy as the Wawaties' dwelling, this place is much better than my lean-to by the bluff. I could stay here all winter, if I had to. Mind you, I won't have to. Surely my family will come looking for me here. I've been here before. That much I know. They must know it, too.

I run my hand along the square timber post, surprised to feel so many nicks and notches. Names, actually. The post is covered in them, *Danny, Jack, Andrew, Pierre*—one must be mine. Being here is bound to stoke my memory.

My stomach gurgles and I realize I haven't eaten since

Mahingan and I grabbed a few strips of dried moose meat on our trek yesterday. Maybe the pots and kettles stacked by the fire pit hold something worth eating. I check under their lids. Empty. Then I spy a small lid, half buried in the fire pit's sand. Kneeling, I unearth it to find, not just a lid, but a whole pot of baked beans beneath it. Buried treasure if I ever saw it! I pull out the small pot and scoop two handfuls of beans to my mouth. Stone cold they are, but mighty delicious just the same. Rummaging around the pots and pans, I soon find a wooden spoon. I've half of the pot finished and I'm sorely tempted to down the lot, but I decide to save the rest for later. I dig a hole closer to the fire and fill it with some of the embers before re-burying the pot. Come dinner, I'll have a heaping of hot, sand-baked beans and, with the luck I'm having, I may even snag a bit of meat to go with it.

I spend the day roaming the area, but there's no hunting to be had. Maybe the animals are smart enough to hide. Maybe they're just not there anymore. I suppose it takes a lot of meat to feed the bellies that fill all those bunk beds.

Though there's been a few snowfalls since the place was emptied, it isn't hard to see the roads leading in and out of the bush. I follow a few and find myself in one of many emptied glades, surrounded by hundreds of snow-covered stumps. *They cut the trees here.* I turn and follow the path down to a leveled clearing. *And then carried—no, dragged them here by horse, I imagine.* I kick the spongy ground beneath the dusting of snow, unearthing shorn bark, and curled shavings. My heart skips. *I'm right. I am!* After so many days of so many questions, answers are as satisfying as ten kettles of baked beans.

And over there is where the logs were squared, stacked, and stored to wait for the spring thaw. Common sense, really, but I can almost see the mountain of timbers piled four men high. Almost hear the ax and saws, and that damned timber stamp marking each end. *Chink. Chink. Chink.* Pulling off my gloves, I look at my callused hands. *That was my job, stamping the hundreds and hundreds of log ends.* My body remembers even if my mind is unsure.

I'm almost running now, chasing the skid road as its wide path slopes and cuts through the thick woods to the river's edge. *The log drive. We started here. I remember! The foreman said the thaw had come—it was time to run the river.* I race to the side of the clearing. *Here ... I was standing here, watching the mighty logs roll down the slope and thunder into the water.* Yearning ripples through me and I know that, although I had the best vantage point, 'twasn't watching I wanted to be doing. I wanted to be in there, shoulder to shoulder with them. A real log driver.

Don't you have some pots to scrub, Bébite?

The voice is so clear I glance around, but there's no one there.

Shut yer gob, Pierre, my answer echoes in reply. I see it all, playing before me, like a waking dream. Pierre tousling my hair. Me shoving him away. And his laugh, that Godforsaken braying forever in my ears. That Pierre, he was a right jackass. He had a few years and muscles on me and he never let me forget it. How many times I'd heard his laughter at my expense. *Hey, everyone, look at Bébite. He wants to wield a broadax and he can't even handle a potato peeler ... You're too small, Bébite ... Leave the work to the real men and get back in the kitchen.* I'd show him. I'd bloody show them all.

A crow caws atop a lone pine before taking flight. I stand in the cold, empty clearing. As quickly as it came, the glimpse of memory fades and I can recall nothing more. Turning, I trudge towards the shanty, but the wide road seems so much longer on the way back. The answers I've wanted for so long have only given me more questions. Two in particular.

Was my father one of the loggers?

Why can't I remember him?

I see Pierre, hear his laugh and that annoying French nickname *Bébite*—"little bug." I can even recall scrubbing those pots, peeling spuds, and stamping log end after log end like it was just a few weeks ago. Indeed, it probably was. I remember all that but, try as I might, all the rest of that day and well into the night, I toss and turn, for I remember neither my father nor what happened next.

How did I show them all? What was I going to do?

Or, more importantly, what have I done?

I wonder if that is why they left me behind.

Chapter 22

*M*y ears ring as I stumble again, gasping from the ache in my side, sick from my spinning head. *Mick? Mick!*

I glance around but there's no sign of him. He was behind me ... right behind. *What happened to him?*

He's not ashore with me and he's not clinging to the floating logs that ride the explosion's dying ripples. Which means he can only be one place. Shantymen now scurry along the shifting timbers, flailing for balance like tightrope walkers as they search the frigid water's dark surface. From shore, I can see there's no sign of Mick between those bobbing logs.

This wasn't supposed to happen. I was going to break up the jam, chop the key log. I was going to show them all, and they'd be telling stories about me just like I was Big Joe Mont-ferrand—but the timber shifted and I got stuck. No matter how I yanked, I could not free my leg. That's when I saw the men running for the shore. That's when I knew they'd freed the key log. The whole thing was going to blow any second. I was about to die.

But Mick appeared beside me. Came out of nowhere and, wedging a cant-hook under the log, he freed me. We bolted for the shore, scrambling from log to log. He was right behind me. Right behind.

Dear God, I scan the black water, please let him be all right.

A man shouts from out on the river. Others join him, scuttling from timber to timber, as easily as running a country road. They grab something with their hooks—it looks like Mick. I pray it is. But someone yells as the logs shift and the men, unable to drag Mick free, push him back under as the timbers collide. They've saved him from a crushing. Still, every man knows Mick will not survive in that water much longer. He has only seconds left, if that. Didn't Benoît tell us how freezing water can douse a man's spirit as quickly as it can a roaring fire? No wonder only the brave few volunteer to free the logjams.

That's why I had to do it. I had to. Only everything went wrong. And now—

I see him then. They drag his full form up onto the log where he flops like a load of wet laundry. He's not moving. One man grabs his feet, another under his arms and they run for shore. Benoît meets them, spreads a blanket on the ground, but moments after Mick's limp body is laid upon it, 'tis sodden in blood. Benoît works quickly, bandaging what he can with what little he has. From his gushing head to the gash in his side, never mind the deathly gray of his skin, Mick's battered body tells me he's dead. But the way Benoît fusses, the way he hastily binds the wounds, despite his own mangled hand, makes me think there is a chance. There has to be.

"Is he—" I grasp Benoît's arm.

Pierre shoves me back. "You did this! First my father's hand … and now—" He lunges for me, but the men hold him back.

"Shirt! Give me a shirt!" Benoît orders, and I throw down my jacket and yank off my plaid shirt. Snatching it, Benoît gingerly wraps it around Mick's head before ordering two men to lift Mick into the back of the wagon as he hops up front. He grabs the reins in his good left hand, pinching them between his remaining right thumb and finger. With a snap, the wagon jolts forward and quickly disappears into the thick spruce. I turn to find every man's gaze upon me. 'Twas all I ever wanted, only not like this.

No one speaks. Their steely glares say enough as they size up this pathetic boy, quivering in his tattered undershirt. I'm no hero. No lumberman. I'm not even a good cookee. I'm a fool, is all. 'Twill be a long road traveled before I earn a sliver of their respect.

"Right, lads," the foreman calls from behind, "them timbers

won't drive themselves."

One by one, the men walk away. But I don't see them leave. I can't take my eyes off the red slush. So much blood. Mick's blood. Shivering, I pick up my coat, hold it in my trembling hands. I should put it on, should try to warm up—but this winter chill is nothing compared to the cold inside me.

My best friend is surely dead. And I killed him.

CHAPTER 23

"Mick!" I waken with a gasp, like I'm coming up from the dark depths. In a cold sweat, I launch myself from the bunk and, bending over, retch into an empty pot. Flinging the door open, I stumble onto the stoop, but there isn't enough air in the whole wide sky. I can't catch my breath and my heart is choking me. I'm drowning, drowning in guilt. Head spinning, I fall back against the log wall.

Dear God, it can't be true. It can't!

I grab a handful of snow and rub my face raw. But no matter how I blink and squint, the sight of his bloodied gray face lingers and burns like bile.

I did this. I killed Mick.

Memories of him flicker past like shuffled cards. Mick and I hired by the foreman. *Cookees for now, Mick, but, sure, we'll be felling and hawing in no time. You'll see.* The excitement of our long ride into the bush. Snowball fights after the first snowfall. *Mick, ye couldn't hit a barn if yer life depended on it. Ye never could.* Mick's wide-mouthed grin, gaping from the bunk above, as he dropped yet another bean-stink upon me. Songs and stories shared in firelight. Plans for our next big adventure. Mick dragging my sleepy arse out of bed on those midnight mornings to help Cook get the breakfast going for the men, or walking miles into the timber limits to bring them their lunches. From ice-in to ice-out, he never once complained—not about the early rising, or bitter cold, not about the endless chores and thankless work, fetching water, chopping wood, peeling spuds. I wanted more adventure, more praise, but Mick, he always did whatever needed doing. Even if it meant cleaning the mess I often made of things. *Don't worry*, he'd say, *I'll take care of it.* And he did, too. Even when Benoît got hurt.

Trapped in a net of memories, one leads me to another, stringing my mind around its many holes. Benoît's hand. Another day I'd sooner forget.

Don't be such a chicken, Mick. I'm just trying it once. I stole a swing of that broadax but somehow lost my grip. We watched it fly, spinning in a perfect arc before sticking in the log where Benoît sat eating the lunch we'd brought. He'd rested his hand on the log as he leaned. Never saw the ax coming.

Just like that, it bit into bark and bone, severing three fingers on his right hand. I saw them. Three bloody sausages in the white snow. They didn't look like fingers at all and I couldn't stop staring at them. Mick had Benoît's hand iced and bound in seconds. He half carried the old man all the way back to the shanty and spent most of the next few weeks taking care of him. Getting him food. Changing his bandages. Or just listening to the same stories over and over again. He forgot all about me. Didn't care that Pierre, Benoît's son, was out for revenge. *It's just three fingers*, I said, when Pierre cornered me in the shanty, accusing me of making his family suffer. Pierre told me that without those fingers, Benoît couldn't swing an ax. And without work, his brothers and sisters would starve. Pierre swore he'd get even. I could tell by his eyes, he meant it.

Mick followed Benoît around like a puppy and, as the old man relearned his timber trade with his left hand, he taught Mick everything he knew. *Mick*. It should have been me. Mick didn't care if he ever left the kitchen. But I was made for lumbering. I begged them to teach me. But Benoît said no. No one, not one man, would let me near his ax or saw. I'd been cursed. Shunned. They didn't invite me to join them while they ate the lunch I'd made and lugged through the woods. They no longer asked me to play my whistle at the fire. As the pile of felled timber grew, so did my lonely work of timber stamping. Hammer in hand, I stamped every bloody log another man felled. Hundreds of them. Day after day. *I didn't come here for this. I came to make my mark.*

And when those logs jammed up, I knew in that moment, my time had come.

CHAPTER 24

I take a deep breath, let the cold night air scour all that's been stirred up inside me. But there's more I need to know, more I don't want to see. My head feels like it might explode with the pressure of the dammed memories. But this place has trenched my mind and, like it or not, the cold truth is gushing out.

Shivering, I wrap my blanket around me and sit on one of the square beams framing the fire pit. I can see them all in my mind's eye, every one of the forty-six men I'd lived with these past few months. I know their bunks, their stories, the way they take their tea, black and "strong enough to float an ax." I can almost see them telling those tales around the pit, sweaters airing overhead, suspenders shucked, socked feet propped and thawing by the fire as pipe smoke filters from their bushy mustaches. I can almost feel the floorboards thumping to the fiddle as they danced at a Saturday night clog. Lord, I wanted to be like them. Big and burly. With more scars than I could count, each with a story wilder than the last.

Yet, not one of those forty-six faces is the man from my dream. The man I know is my da. He wasn't here. I'm sure of it. He's not looking for me, because he doesn't even know I'm missing. I take comfort in that. It makes sense. Why else wouldn't a father keep searching for his son?

I rub my hands together and hold them out before the fire. *Still, someone knows I'm here. These shantymen—surely they know I've been left behind.*

I made mistakes, I admit that. But these men had children of their own. I can't believe they'd just go off and leave me. They wouldn't, would they?

It's a dangerous place, the bush. Pierre's voice returns, unbidden, calling up another memory. Only we weren't in the shanty. This time, he'd cornered me out in the woods. I'd run off after the men left me at the water's edge. After what happened to Mick. I didn't want any of them to see the tears drawing cold lines down my face, but Pierre had followed.

Leave me be, Pierre. Fear filled my voice and chest. I glanced around the clearing, but I knew no one was there. The drive had started, and the men were on the river.

Do you know how long I have waited for this? First my father's hand and now Mick. He shoved me and I landed hard on my backside.

Stop, Pierre, don't—

Without warning, his boot hit me in the gut, knocking out wind and words. I had to get out of there. Rolling to my stomach, I started to crawl, scrabbling at the coarse snow with red-raw hands. *If I could just make it to the trees,* I thought, *I might be able to—*

Pierre grabbed my hair and yanked me to my feet. *It's time you paid, Bébite.* He swung his fist, catching my cheek. Light exploded around me, followed by a searing throb, as though his fist were a blacksmith's iron and not mere flesh and bone. My head rang like a struck anvil. Pierre pounded my side and I crumpled, but it did nothing to block the next blow. Or the next.

I ... didn't do ... I didn't mean ... the words escaped in wet gasps through blood, tears, spit, and snot.

You think you're a real man, eh, little Bébite? You will have to learn to fight better than this. With a grunt, he punched my side once more, reveling in my pain. Grabbing my collar, he dragged me to a stand and rested his hand on my shoulder as he considered what to do next. *Me, I should kill you now and be done with it. No one would miss you. It's a dangerous place, the bush. People die out here all the time.*

From my swelling eye, I glanced at the bluff's edge one step behind me, at the rocky ground nearly fifteen feet below. *I could jump,* I thought, trying to convince myself. I looked back at Pierre. His eyes were hard, resolute. He'd made his decision. Whatever it was, 'twas surely bad for me.

Pierre tightened his grip on my collar and cocked his other fist. Just as he was about to launch his knuckled cannonball at me, I kicked up my legs and threw out my arms, shoving off with whatever strength I had left. The force of it exploded between us and Pierre staggered back a few paces, as did I, but one step from the edge was all I had. Limbs flailing, I dropped over the bluff, slowly at first, as though floating, before slamming the ground with the force of a felled timber. It crushed all breath from me and I lay there gasping, mouth sucking vainly like a cod tossed ashore.

Pierre's head appeared over the ledge. He seemed miles above. *Your stupidity will kill you sooner or later,* his voice echoed. He hesitated for a moment—maybe he was thinking of coming down to help me or finish me. Either way, he simply left.

It started to snow, then, as I lay there fighting to breathe. Fighting to live. And I realized that I did not want to fight anymore. The shantymen were on the river. They couldn't stop the drive to look for a runaway cookee even if they wanted to. And who would want to look for me, anyway? Darkness seeped into the edges of my vision, as I watched the white flakes float towards me. *Like angel feathers,* I thought, amazed by their numbing touch. But if there was an angel, I never saw it, for the darkness soon spilled over, and all went black.

CHAPTER 25

The ax bites into the log and sticks there, and I raise them both overhead before slamming them to the ground. The force of it wedges the blade deeper and deeper until, finally, the wood splinters. Picking up the bits, I toss them on the log pile. I don't really need more firewood, but there's something about chopping that helps me think. Or maybe, it just keeps my mind off things long enough for me to calm down. Either way, I'm sweating in my shirtsleeves, bashing the bejaysus out of the logs, and it feels good. Real good. I'm so into it I don't even hear Mahingan coming.

"Did you chop all of that?" he asks.

The sound makes me jump and the blade skips off the log, just missing my leg.

"Don't sneak up on me like that!" I blurt. "I nearly cut my foot off. *Jaysus*, can't you just walk up like a normal person?"

He folds his arms and tilts his head. "Can't you just use your ears like a normal person?" He juts his jaw towards the log pile. "Did you chop all that?"

I nod. So, I didn't do it all today, but 'twas me that chopped it when the camp was up and running. I vented back here often, it seems. Still, I let him think it's my afternoon's work.

"Come back to yell at me some more?" I say, taking another log and setting it on the stump I use for a chopping block.

Mahingan shrugs.

"How's your arm?"

"*Mishomis* says I should get the use of these fingers back, but I need to be—"

"Patient?" I finish for him. I didn't realize the gash had injured his grip. It reminds me of Benoît. I spit in my hands, go back to my chopping.

"*Mishomis* says to invite you to eat with us tonight. We're having the beaver I caught." He clenches his jaw. "I mean ... we caught."

This boy is nothing like the one that went storming out of here the other day. He seems deflated. Smaller. I wonder what else his grandfather has been saying to him. Mind you, I'm not the same boy he left, thanks to the few memories I've unearthed.

"He says it is time," Mahingan continues. "He wants to talk with you about who you are."

I glance at him over my shoulder. "I already know more than I want to know about that."

Mahingan frowns. This wasn't the answer he expected. "He wants to tell you about the Wolf."

I pause mid-swing. I never told Mahingan about my wolf encounters. "What about the wolf?"

"I don't know; he didn't tell me. The message is for you."

"What message?"

Mahingan speaks loud and slow as if I can't hear. "I do not know. He did not tell me."

I'm hungry for a good feed, but no meal is worth this frustration. "How do you even know about the wolf?"

"It is my kin." He folds his arms and his chest puffs up a bit. "My father gave me this name, *Mahingan*. It means Wolf."

I wonder how much he knows about my wolf visits. "Were you spying on me the night I touched it?"

"You *touched* it?" he says, in disbelief.

"Yes." It feels amazing to finally tell someone, even if it is Mahingan.

"But how ... you're not even *Anishnaabe* ... you don't even know ..." His voice rises with frustration.

"So," I say, "you did come to yell some more."

"No," says he, catching himself. "I came to invite you to eat with us. I did what I was asked. Come or don't come. It is no difference to me." He turns and starts walking away.

A warm meal. My mouth waters. All this chopping has worked up a right appetite. "I don't even know how to find your home."

"I do," he calls back over his shoulder, not missing a beat.

I swing the ax once more, wedging the blade into the stump, and, grabbing my coat, run after him.

CHAPTER 26

Their bark-covered home is not far from the shanty. I'm surprised I'd never come across it before. On the way, Mahingan tells me it's one of many places they use while hunting. "We build the smaller *pikogan* for shelter—it's light and sturdy, perfect for traveling on the traplines. *Mishomis* and I have only a few more traps to check before going home to our main winter camp."

When I ask, he tells me his mother, sisters, and baby brother stay in that camp from October to March, along with his aunts and little cousins.

"They keep the camp running. Waiting for the men to return with game. But every year, it seems there is less and less hunting to be had. I worry that, like many other *Anishnaabeg,* soon we will not have enough to eat." His shoulders slump slightly. "I hope my uncles and cousins hunting along our other family traplines are having more success," he adds.

The many clear-cut glades around the shanty come to

mind and I wonder if that's where he hunted before. But I don't ask.

"Is your father with them?" I say.

Mahingan pauses for a moment, but he doesn't look at me. "My father died six months ago." Head down, he picks up his pace, a clear sign that this conversation is over.

My heart goes out to him. He must miss him terribly. I miss mine, too. But at least when I get out of these never-ending woods, I'll see my father again.

Grandfather welcomes us in to his *pikogan*. Small as it is, I'm glad of it, for the wind's chill is picking up, cutting through my coat like a blade fresh from the grindstone. The sky, now slate gray, hangs low and heavy. Even I can tell 'tis full of flurries. I'll not be tarrying long, not if I want to get back to the shanty before the storm.

He's already laid out a small feast. A few baskets of dried berries, a bowl of orange mush—squash, I think, or pumpkin. From the center of the *pikogan*, meat dangles on a long rope over the fire. 'Tis the beaver, all right. Shed of its skin, strung up by its back legs, it slowly spins on the rope's unwinding twist. Whatever guilt I had is gone as I smell it roasting. My stomach growls, my mouth slathered, wet as the dripping meat.

Grandfather checks it and, satisfied, unties the rope. He carves off a few pieces and sets them aside in a smaller bowl.

Mahingan's stomach gurgles on the other side of me, but he doesn't make a move. Doesn't dig in. So neither will I. Bloody torture is what it is.

Then the old man takes a scoop from each bowl and basket and fills the smaller dish. I hold out my hands as he turns to me with it, but he passes right by and leans over the fire, stopping to scrape the *whole* lot into the flames. I glance at Mahingan, for surely he's as shocked as I, but neither of them seems to notice me. Grandfather takes a pinch of tobacco and throws it in over the burning food. He's mad, well and truly. I'm sure of it.

"We thank *Kichi Manido*, Creator, for giving us this food, by giving some back," he says, not looking at me. My face burns—for he's read my mind.

"Like saying Grace?" I ask.

"If we are not thankful, why should we be given more?"

He has a point. I never thought of it like that.

He hands Mahingan a small knife and the boy near leaps out of his seat to cut a hunk for himself. I follow suit, pulling my knife from my pocket and slicing a wedge of the hot meat, eat it right off the back of the blade.

Dear God in heaven, it's good!

By the time the meal is done, I swear Mahingan's belly is two sizes larger. Mine surely feels it. His greasy face slips into a grin and I can't help but smile back.

CHAPTER 27

After the meal, Mahingan's grandfather carves the remaining meat and sets it aside for smoking. Then, removing the animal's skull, he ties it together with the bones of its feet and gives the unusual collection to Mahingan, who takes it outside. I figure it's for the dog. Slipping on my coat, I follow him, but he heads away from the dog, stopping in front of a slender birch tree a few yards from the *pikogan*. As I approach, I notice dozens of animal skulls and bones dangling from the white branches.

Mahingan ties the beaver bones alongside the others with such reverence, it feels like we're in a church and not outdoors. Or maybe the outdoors is his church.

Without its flesh and fur, the beaver's orangey incisors seem nearly twice as long. I stare at them as the breeze rattles the skull among the bones. "Those are some teeth," I say.

"Some teeth," Mahingan echoes, flexing his injured arm.

"I still can't believe you caught that with your bare hands."

He stands in silence for a few moments, reminding me of his grandfather. "My father taught me. He showed me many things about hunting," he says, stepping back from the birch. "He taught me to always thank the animal whose life keeps us living."

"So why do you hang up its bones?" I say. "Why not give it to the dog?"

His look turns on me so fast I think I was wrong to ask. I didn't mean any disrespect; I just wondered is all.

"We give it back to the forest, to honor the beaver. It's the way our ancestors have done it for thousands of years. So that the beaver will continue to allow themselves to be caught by us."

I don't really have a reply to that. It doesn't make sense that a beaver or any animal would give its life on purpose. Still, if his people have been doing this for generation after generation, who am I to question it? Maybe they know something I don't.

We return to the shelter and settle by the fire. Grandfather lights a pipe and stares off, deep in thought. Though I should be getting on my way, the warmth and glow is too inviting. Even the smell of the tobacco comforts me. I'm in no rush to go back to the big, empty shanty or to learn what other memories it holds in its cold shadows. And so we wait, Mahingan and me, while his grandfather teaches us patience once more. Finally, he speaks.

"Learn from the Wolf." He stops, draws on his pipe.

I settle in, ready to get his wisdom, but after five minutes go by, it seems that is all he's going to say. I slip off my belt and, using my knife, carve a small beaver and an axe to remind me of the shanty. But long after I've finished, Grandfather still does not speak.

Finally, after an eternity of silence, I have to ask. "What do you mean? How will I learn from a wolf? Does it know my family? Or where I live? Or my name?" I mean it as a joke, but no one laughs.

"You do ask too many questions," Grandfather states.

Mahingan snorts.

Is this why he brought me here? What sort of message is this?

"Mahingan said you were going to tell me about who I am," I challenge. I don't mean to sound rude. I'm only stating the truth.

Grandfather nods at Mahingan who begins to speak. "Remember the day on the ice?"

How could I forget? My bones ache with the very thought of that cold water.

"I was looking at your fishing hole and the ice broke and I fell in. I would have died if it weren't for you, Mahingan." It occurs to me that I never did thank him for that.

"I didn't save you," he says, and I can't tell if he's sorry or proud of it. "I yelled at you to get off the ice. The weather had been too warm; the ice was too thin." He doesn't mention the snowball or the insults. Mind you, he also leaves out the fact that I was poaching. Fishing on his claim.

"I saw you go under," Mahingan continues, "but you were too far out for me to reach you with a branch and I did not trust the ice. Then, as I stood on the shore, I heard him coming. Paws pounding the snow, panting, growing nearer and nearer as he raced up from behind. The Wolf ran right past me and out onto the ice. Splaying his legs wide and crouching low, he crawled to where you'd disappeared. When you came up that one last time, he grabbed your sleeve in his jaws and jerked and jerked until he'd dragged you out."

At first, I think Mahingan's only teasing, but there's no hint of humor on him, and even Grandfather Wawatie nods as though Mahingan speaks true. I wonder whether Mahingan would have saved me or, like Pierre, left me for dead in my own mess. I honestly can't say for sure what he would have done. Nor would do, were it to happen again. But I feel he's telling the truth.

As crazy as it sounds, that wolf saved me, so he did. Though I've no idea why.

CHAPTER 28

Grandfather Wawatie tells Mahingan to walk me back to the shanty. I want to say I can find my own way home, but, truth be told, I can't. Much as I hate taking it, I need Mahingan's help. But as we start walking into the dark woods, I begin to wonder if I might have been better on my own. For Mahingan's of a mind to spook me, so he is. And with an imagination like mine, it doesn't take much before I'm one scare away from wetting myself. Though I'd never tell him that. Not in a million years.

"What's that?" he says, stopping again, his dark eyes shifting side to side. "Did you hear it?"

I freeze. Listen to the sound of my breath. Twigs snap in the distance, but I can't tell if it's from cold or footsteps. Even the shadows play tricks on me, showing me what's not there.

Mahingan glances at the moon disappearing behind the gray clouds. "The *Windigo* will surely be on the prowl this night."

"*Windigo,*" says I, as hooked as a hungry trout. "What's that?"

"The *Windigo* towers above the tallest man, but is as gaunt as a skeleton," Mahingan answers, his eyes wide. "It smells of death and decay, for that is what it brings as it seeks to feed its never-ending hunger."

"An animal?" I've never seen one like that before.

"No, a *Manido*. A spirit." The wind whistles in the trees, rattling their dead branches. "And the more it eats," Mahingan continues, "the bigger it gets. But as it grows, so does its hunger."

I lick my lips, surprised my mouth has gone so dry. "What does it eat?"

"Humans," Mahingan answers. "It attacks, devouring flesh and bone, drinking hot blood while its prey screams. Many people die of fright, just from the sight of it coming—they say they are the lucky ones."

I can see it all as clear as though 'twere happening right before me. Almost hear the shrieking.

"It hunts in the dead of winter on nights like this." Mahingan pauses. "Victims know it's coming by the smell, the air growing colder, the blizzard stirring up right before it attacks."

I swallow.

Satisfied with my obvious terror, despite my best efforts to hide it, Mahingan starts to walk again.

He's messing with me. Telling ghost stories. Surely, he is. "I don't believe you. There's no such thing—"

"When you fell through the ice," Mahingan interrupts, stopping to face me, "did you feel the *Mishibeshi* trying to pull you deeper into the water?"

My mouth drops. I did feel something dragging me down, gulping me into darkness.

"Things exist," Mahingan continues, "whether you believe in them or not."

Snow swirls between us on a sudden chilly gust. I catch my breath and look at Mahingan, who glances around nervously. He lowers his voice as though we're being watched. "I have seen the *Windigo* this very winter." His eyes stare back in time. "I was checking our traps, and it was late in the evening, like now. I had one more trap to go. As I approached, I saw a great, hairy thing towering over the dead fox in my snare. I could hear its wet breath from two hundred yards away. It tore through my rope like it was nothing but spiderweb and took my fox. The *Windigo* raided my three traps that night. But I survived. I saw the *Windigo* and lived to tell about it."

I can tell he's not joking. He's as scared as I am now. But that doesn't make me feel any better. In fact, it makes me more afraid.

"Let's go," he looks over his shoulder. "The sooner I get you back to the shanty, the sooner I'll be sleeping by my fire."

As we approach the shanty, it crosses my mind to invite him in. The wind is picking up and besides, there is lots of room. He'd have his pick of fifty bunks. Annoying as he is, I wouldn't mind the company. But I don't bother asking, not after his last reaction to the shanty. Mahingan doesn't tarry, either. The shanty comes into view and I step past Mahingan, but before I can turn back to say goodnight, he's gone. Were it not for the fir branches rustling from his passing, I'd hardly know he'd been there at all.

CHAPTER 29

Inside, I stoke the fire I'd banked that afternoon, get it good and blazing. All that silly talk of ice monsters and winter ghouls has chilled me to the core, so it has. Even though I'm soon sweating, I keep adding log after log. I like the light, if not the heat. Everyone knows them specters keep to the shadows.

I don't recall falling asleep, but something wakens me. The fire has settled to its orange embers and the wind is whistling over chimney hole. But, over its low moan, I hear another sound, one that rivets me to the spot. A cough. 'Tis outside in the dark, a fair ways away, maybe by the tree line. But I heard it just the same. I wait, heart thumping, and just as I think I may have dreamt it, I hear it once more. Closer this time. Not a bark, or a howl, but a gagging, wet and phlegmy.

I have to see, even though 'tis the last thing I want to do. Crawling around the bunks, I creep my way to the one window by the door and peek over the sill. Frost blurs the view, so I lay my hot hand upon the icy glass, melting a small handprint. Through the palm, I see it. All seven feet of it. For a great, shaggy beast is tromping from the darkness, heading straight towards the shanty!

The *Windigo!*

I duck down, sure it can hear my heart pulsing.

I have to get out of here! Now! But the only door faces the oncoming creature. *I'm trapped—there's no way out.* My mind scrabbles as my eyes search the room. *No way out ... but up. The chimney!*

A wide square hole is cut into the roof just over the large fire pit. It's bigger than a normal chimney. *But is it big enough for me?* Running and hopping on the timber frame, I clamber up the post and leap for the chimney opening, only to find a cover, like a small table, propped over the hole. I heave against it and it gives, sliding onto the roof. Snow rains upon me, hissing in the fire below, but the rattle of the front door latch is all I can hear. With a desperate pump of my legs, I push and pull myself through the opening and onto the snow-covered roof. Lying on my stomach, gripping the chimney ledge to keep me from slipping off the steep slope, I hear the creature enter the shanty. Breath ragged and soggy, it staggers across the wood floor, stopping at my bunk.

It's looking for me!

Through the square hole, I can see its shaggy back as it bends and pulls aside my blanket, grumbling as it tosses it into the fire. The blanket smolders, sending dark smoke up the chimney. The cloud stings my eyes and I'm terrified that I'll have to cough, so I shove my face in the snow beneath me. Moments later, the front door slams shut and footsteps crunch through the snow on the far side of the shanty as the creature returns to the woods.

Numb from cold or fear, and probably both, I wait for ages before moving. I don't want to get down, but I can't stay up here. I'll die of cold on this roof. Finally, I let go of the chimney opening and slide to the roof's edge, dropping into the drift below. Trembling uncontrollably, I go back into the shanty and roll the biggest barrel in front of the door. 'Twouldn't stop that seven-foot monster—still, I feel better having it there. The shanty is filled with dark smoke from my burning blanket and an unfamiliar smell of something rancid hangs in the air. I bury the blanket's singed end in the sand before throwing some wood on the fire. I want to run away. To hide. And I can't stop shaking. Not even after I've taken off my wet clothes and wrapped myself in another blanket. Every shiver stirs up another question.

Should I try and find the Wawaties' place?
Is it headed there now?
What if it comes back?

106   TIMBER WOLF

Think, now. Think.

This is the safest place to be.

Why would it come back?

The shaking slows. My breathing steadies and my teeth stop their chatter. But not my mind.

Maybe it wasn't a Windigo.

Maybe it was a logger come back to look for me.

The thought that I've missed my rescuer disturbs me, but something tells me that whatever it was, 'twas more foe than friend.

There's no proof 'tis me that's here. I'll be fine—

But the thought is cut short when my eyes turn to the icy window. For there's my handprint, a clear view on the dark night beyond. And if that weren't bad enough, there just above, is another massive handprint; its mangled fingers, webbed, warped, and anything but human, burned into the frost.

CHAPTER 30

I don't sleep at all the rest of that long night. With first
light, I'm up and dressed and ready to find the Wawaties.
The snow is falling in big flakes, with no sign of letting
up. But I have to talk to Mahingan. Maybe they know how to
protect against further *Windigo* attacks. I set off through the
woods at a good clip. I have a fair idea of which way their
shelter lies, now that it's daytime, and, sure enough, I find
their camp. Or what *was* their camp. The place is empty,
stripped. Even the *pikogan* is just a bare frame, a skeleton
of saplings.

The Windigo! It got them!

My imagination starts running away on me, but soon
enough I rein it in. The structure stands, but the bark cov-
erings are gone. Not torn or burned, just missing. There are
no signs of Mahingan or his grandfather—even their snowshoes and toboggan are gone. Surely their dog would have
attacked the creature, and yet there is no blood on the snow,
no sign of a struggle.

Calm yourself. Didn't Mahingan say they had a few more places to check on the trapline before going back to their main winter camp?

I heave a sigh of relief. They aren't dead, just gone.

Gone. The weight of it sinks in and, once again, I feel abandoned. They didn't even say goodbye. Or good riddance, which is more like something Mahingan might say. His grandfather never told me who I was, which way I'd find a town, or even if there was one. I look at the tracks left by their snowshoes and sled, slowly filling with fresh flakes. I could try to follow them, but if I don't find them before the tracks are buried, I'll be back where I started two weeks ago, with no food, no shelter, and no idea where I am.

So, now what?

My stomach grumbles in reply. I need to eat. Build up my strength and maybe, when the snow lets up, I'll follow the river. If the logs can follow the river to the town, surely I can, too. I feel better with a plan. Scattered as it is, at least it's something.

Back at the shanty, I scavenge for materials. I can picture the snare and know exactly how to make it. Surely, I've made these a hundred times back home. Wherever home is. A bit of rummaging turns up a length of rope in one of the barrels back at the shanty and two straight lengths of branch as thick as my wrist. I spend the morning cutting a stick into two-foot-length stakes and whittling the other to a white point. You never know when a spear might come in handy.

Lugging spear, stakes, and rope back into the woods, to a sapling near a thicket, I shove the stakes into the ground in a foot-wide circle and use the thinnest one as an arch at the opening. The noose goes there. Using my knife, I trim the sapling's branches, bend it and secure it to the noose, careful not to spring the trap myself. Any rabbit coming along here that happens to stick its head in there is mine. Mind you, I haven't any bait.

What sort of animal would be dumb enough to be lured by curiosity alone?

The bundle of remaining sticks lies buried by the thickly falling snow. I dig them out and pile them in my arms before trudging off in search of another thicket. I've enough for three traps. Surely, one will catch my dinner. But if the snow keeps falling at this rate, all traps and hope will soon be buried.

As I kneel at the next thicket, my neck prickles. Something's watching me. I pivot quickly, half expecting to see the *Windigo* mid-pounce, but 'tis only the wolf standing about a hundred yards away.

"You scared the bejaysus out of me!" I say, relieved to see him, for many reasons. Maybe he's watching over me, or maybe he's lonely. Either way, he's company. He sits and observes me driving the stakes into the ground. "Don't worry, this isn't for wolf," I say, "just rabbit. You like rabbit, don't you?"

He yawns. A great tongue-curling grin. He's alone, as usual.

"Where's your pack?" I ask. He tilts his head at my question, then raises his brow, as though asking me the very same. I laugh. The sound of it makes him bark as he pitches his rump in the air, head down between his paws, ready to play. Had I a ball, I'd toss it for him. I find it odd that I'd felt so afraid of him those first nights. Here in the daylight, he seems like a gangly pup. A year or two old, if that.

Snare set, I pick up the sticks for the last one and walk deeper into the woods, turning to see if the wolf is following. Sure enough, he is. He's not coming too close, preferring to stay a safe distance away. Still, I like having him around, watching over me. Listening to me. But, as we approach another clearing, he stops. Barks once. This time it's not for play.

I smell the meat before I see it. Fresh kill. Like the wolf, I sniff the cold air for other scents, wary of running into another hungry hunter. If this animal smells the meat, so will others. Bigger ones, with fangs and claws. But the air is clean, crisp. No scent of anything but the meat.

That should have been my first warning.

CHAPTER 31

Any hesitation is washed away by the slather in my mouth. Meat. Real meat and lots of it. I can almost taste it, almost feel the greasy juice of it running down my chin. I press on through the thicket of branches, following the tangy smell. And there it is. The bloodied carcass lies over a thick branch about eight feet from the ground above a small clearing. A deer, I'd say. A small one, about fifty pounds, though it's hard to tell from the mass of black feathers frantically flapping around the haunch of meat. After days of nothing but scraps here and there, I could cry at the sight.

"Oh, Wolf, we'll be having a right feed tonight!"

The crows eye me warily as they rip what they can. They knew a bigger predator would arrive. As do I. 'Tis the way of the woods.

The wolf whinges and licks his lips as he looks at the meat.

He wants it, too. But he'll not step a paw into the clearing. Instead, he circles halfway around and back, pacing side to side. The snow spreads before us like a great rumpled sheet, unmarked except for the bloodied slush beneath the deer. No footprints, yet. I look behind me. We have to act fast.

"Come on, then," I say, taking a step.

The wolf whines, his worried eyes darting between me and the deer.

"You're not afraid of a few mangy birds, are ye?" I throw down the stakes and wave my spear over my head as I step in closer. The crows reluctantly leave their feed and settle themselves in the nearby branches, but a few hungry stragglers remain, frantically pecking what they can. But the wolf won't move from the edge. Perhaps the height of the meat frustrates him. For no wolf-sized animal can reach it. I grip my spear in both hands and move closer to the deer. A few good jabs with this would surely free it.

The wolf barks twice.

"Whisht, now," I turn and scold. "Don't worry yourself. I'll share it ... even though you're too afraid to get it. But must you call every animal in God's kingdom?"

He shrinks for a moment at the harshness in my voice, but he can't stay still as he anxiously paces the edge, whining and whimpering. Something has him riled. I can tell by his flattened ears he's heard nothing to worry him so.

I scan the woods around us. Nothing but trunks and pine. *Does he smell another animal coming? All the more reason to get our prize and go.*

Turning back to the deer, I step in closer. The remaining crows reluctantly give up their find to join the others biding time on higher branches. I feel their beady eyes upon me, but they needn't bother waiting. I'm not planning on leaving any precious meat behind. With the butt end of my spear, I shove the carcass two or three times. It lowers the back end but the deer is good and jammed between the fork of the branches. This isn't going to be as easy as I thought.

How did it get up that far, anyway?

At first, I think it got stuck or impaled itself trying to leap away from some predator. But this is a fairly fresh kill and my footprints are the only ones in the snow. I lean over for a better angle. Maybe I can pry it loose from the front. I study the forelegs and head dangling over the other side of the branch and realize the animal isn't just bloodied from where the scavengers had torn chunks off its rump. From tip to tail, indeed, the whole carcass is bare red flesh. No predator skins its prey. None, other than man. But this was not the Wawaties' way.

"Wolf." I turn to him. "Do you know what this means? Someone *else* put this here. We're saved!"

Wolf whimpers, watching my feet as I circle the deer. He

knows. Knew it the minute we arrived in this clearing. Yet, it is only slowly dawning on me; I've been thinking with my stomach. The lure, the clearing, it all makes sense. I should have realized long before that moment, for I'd spent the afternoon setting up my own traps. I look up at the bloodied carcass a good eight feet in the air. This trap isn't to catch a rabbit. It's meant for something much bigger. Something that eats meat.

A bear.

Reaching for my knife, I grab the lowered back leg of the carcass. The bear could be here any minute, and who knows how long it might be before the trapper returns? All I know for sure is that my wolf and I have to eat. The crows safely scavenged some, why can't we?

The wolf whimpers as I hack at the deer. Careful not to dislodge the body and trip the trap, I cut away a good sized hank, enough to do us for a few days. Surely the trapper will be back by then.

Home. Wherever it is, I'm going home ... and with a full belly. I smile, pleased with myself. "There you are now, ye scavengers," I nod to the black birds eyeing my every move with their jerky heads, "you may have the rest." Prize in hand, I take a step back.

One tiny step.

I never see the razor fangs leaping out of the snow. Their

hungry teeth bite deep and fast, swallowing my leg up to the knee before I can react, before my wolf can utter a sound. Maybe he barked. Maybe I screamed. But I neither see nor hear a thing, for a great wave of pain roars in my ears, drowning all as it drags me under.

Chapter 32

I don't know how long I am out for. I only wish it had been longer. Even before I open my eyes, great stabbing pain shoots in and around my thigh, my whole leg throbs with it.

What ... what happened?

My leg. Great jaws.

The bear?

A wet nose nudges my chin. Snuffles around my face.

I jolt awake, arms flailing as the wolf's hot tongue welcomes me back to the land of the living. To the clearing where I've fallen and still lie beneath the deer carcass in the bloodied snow.

Twilight. I've been out for some time. Raising myself onto one elbow, I glance down at my right leg, mashed and mangled in the metal mouth of a great trap. The snow beneath is stained cherry red. So much blood. My head spins at the sight and throbbing pain of it, and I lie back, covering my eyes.

What an idiot! Why didn't I check the ground? All I had to do was poke it with my spear. Why didn't I listen to the wolf like Grandfather Wawatie said? Instead, I'd let my pride and hunger get the best of me.

Branches snap and the wolf turns, a snarl curling his black lips. Among the thin trunks in the distance, something moves. It stops for a moment, then turning in our direction, lumbers towards us. By the size and shape, I can guess what it is.

A bear.

The gathering of crows launches from the branches above me, their warning cries fading into silence. *Not good. Not good at all. We have to get out of here, fast.*

I try to stand, but there is no way my leg will hold me, and I slump back onto my stomach. Scrabbling in the snow, dragging my injured leg behind me, I move a foot or two towards the wolf as he backs up, but the far edge of the clearing lies a good twenty yards away. As though the trees can save us. As though the bear can't follow my trail of blood.

On the next lunge, a shredding pain rips through my right leg and I cry out. A taut chain about three feet long tethers the steel trap to the ground. Something to keep the wounded prey from escaping. My heart pounds. This wounded prey has reached the end of his line.

The creature comes to a stop in the shadows just beyond the deer. It turns its head to consider the carcass in the tree. Great misty clouds of hot breath hide its face, but even in the dim light, I see the shaggy body stands seven feet tall. Fear grips my stomach tighter than any cold metal trap. I've seen this creature before.

Windigo!

The wolf growls, hackles raised.

"Go!" I pant, as the *Windigo's* head turns from the deer's bloodied body to my own. I shove the wolf hard. "Run, go on!"

But the wolf won't leave me. His loyalty chains him as strongly as any trap. Ears flattened, fur spiked, a growl deep in his throat, he moves his small body between me and the sinister creature. If only the wolf's courage could cut like my knife or jab like my spear, but they lie where they fell in the snow by the deer. I'm defenseless, bloodied, and trapped, with nothing to save me but an angry pup.

The creature takes another look at the deer, slung in the tree. *Dear God in heaven*, I pray, for prayer is all I've left. *Make it go for the easy lure ...*

It is, I realize with horror, as the *Windigo* turns and lumbers towards me.

CHAPTER 33

Within seconds, the beast is upon us. The wolf jumps onto its shoulder, his fangs seeking purchase in the hairy hide, but the beast flings him off. Snarling, the wolf lunges for its legs, its arms; growling and barking, he tears at its fur. I've never seen the wolf so vicious. But this is a fight to the death. We both know it. It crouches, ears back and teeth bared, preparing for another attack, but this time when he leaps, the creature swings its thick arm, meeting the wolf dead on. With a sickening crack, it hits the wolf mid-leap and sends him flying across the clearing.

"No!" I cry, as the wolf's limp body hits the snow and rolls to a dead stop. But the looming creature steps into my view as it heads towards me. 'Tis then I see the bloodied, wooden stick in its grip.

A club? Does a ghost use a weapon?

I raise my eyes to the creature's massive fur head as it trudges towards me, its wet breath heaving and ragged. *What is it, this devil's spawn?* I've no idea but, in the core of my being, I know one thing for sure. *'Tis evil.*

Its great paw reaches up and pulls back its fur ... hood.

"A man?" I shake my head, stunned.

"I was," his voice comes in deep shreds amid his wheezing, "once."

As he steps into the fading light, I see that his features seem contorted, misshapen, wrong. As though his face once melted and cooled, leaving him forever malformed. The right side of his face seems frozen in a wax grimace. Even his hair avoids his gruesome features, retreating off his skull to huddle at the back in long greasy strands. Animal skins hang from his broad shoulders, a shaggy coat of sorts, with a fur-lined hood, belted with a thick rope at his waist. Six leather sheaths hang from his belt, each holding a small knife. The one strapped to his leg runs the length of his shinbone.

What sort of prey demands that kind of a weapon? I swallow. *What sort of a man uses it?*

I flinch as he kneels beside me, but the motion only makes my agony flare. Even the slightest movement causes searing pain in my leg. It burns and blazes as though skewered on a roasting spit turning over a great fire. He pulls off his fur mitts and grips the jaws of the trap in his scarred hands. I whimper, but I know the trap has to come off. In the midst of my pain, I notice then how the fingers on his right hand have melted together, a gelatinous mass of flesh and bone. The handprint on the window!

"You ruined it," he growls through gritted teeth. With his fiendish grin frozen on his face, I can't tell what he's thinking. Then he viciously wrenches the metal jaws apart, ripping its fangs from my flesh. The agony of it shudders through my body and I collapse back onto the snow.

Lord, take me now.

Hot blood gushes from six or seven deep gashes on the front and back of my thigh, soaking my shredded pant leg. He scoops a handful of snow, to staunch it, or perhaps, to cool the burning pain. But instead, he sits back on his haunches using the snow to clean each tooth on his trap.

"No use. No use. It'd smell your blood a mile away." Cursing, he throws the trap on the ground and walks back to the deer. He stops to pick up my knife, raising the blade to admire it in the dim light before running his thumb along its sharp edge. Satisfied, he tucks my knife in his belt with all the others and sucks the blood off his thumb. Whoever that man is, whatever he is, he's no help to us. In fact, he is more dangerous than any animal in the forest. Bears are driven by hunger. They follow their natural instinct. But what dark madness, what twisted instincts guide this man—I don't know. Nor do I want to find out.

"Wolf," I call, pushing myself up to sit. But his body doesn't move. I can't tell if he is living or dead. I have to get to him. We have to get out of here but, first, I need to bandage my leg. Using my scarf, I bind the wounds the best I can, but within seconds, even the scarf is sodden with red. Just the effort of tying it wears me out and I lie back, trying to clear my head.

The man cuts a rope round the back of the tree and lowers the deer onto his shoulder. Then he comes for me.

I want to fight him, to go to my wolf, to get us out of here, but all my strength has seeped into the snow. He reaches for me with those melted hands and I can do nothing. Not even cry for help. But, sure, who will hear me in this endless wood? Slinging me over his other shoulder, he walks past the wolf's still body and I can do nothing. For I am nothing, nothing but another bloodied carcass carried off into the darkness.

CHAPTER 34

I open my eyes to the familiar crackle and snap of a roaring fire. A long knife shifts the blazing logs, exposing their underbellies, making them blush orange-red.

Home.

"Da?"

"I can't do it," a voice wheezes, waking me to this nightmare. The man from the woods. He crouches at the crude hearth—a circle of stones in the middle of the floor—and, resting the tip of the great blade in the embers, turns to the corner. "Don't ask me to."

Who else is here? And where is here?

I lie on the dirt floor of a tiny wooden log shack, a shed, really, for 'tis only eight or nine feet wide and just as long and high. Turning my pounding head, I notice hides of all shapes and sizes cover the walls and a great mound of them lies heaped in the corner. Over what must be the door, the only exit, hangs a thick, brown, shaggy skin. Next to it, on three rough pegs, hang the clothes he'd worn in the clearing: the cloak of skins, the furry leggings, and the belt of knives. The longer blade's sheath, the one I saw strapped to his leg, hangs on a hook all its own.

"You were right. You said he'd come," he whispers, his back to me. Even without the thick coat on, his size amazes me. I glance at the covered doorway and back at his broad shoulders filling the tiny shack. Knives or not, he'll have no trouble keeping me captive.

He looks over his shoulder at me and I see then who he is talking to. On the back wall hang dozens of animal skulls. Rabbits, deer, beaver, and God knows what else. The gathering of their bleached heads unsettles me. I've seen animal skeletons before, in the woods, in Mahingan's tree. I'm sure I've even saved a few bones myself, but not like this. My stomach twists at the sight. For it isn't the skulls that truly unnerve me, just the empty space waiting in the center of them.

"All right! All right! I'll do it." Hushing the silent bones, he stares at me, his frozen grin and vacant gaze as unsettling as their bared teeth and gaping sockets. He rolls up his sleeves, baring his thick forearms. The left is scarred, but not like the white-pink blotches on his hands. Instead, it is seared by fierce red welts, three triangles. He clenches his warped jaw.

His eyes shift to the hilt of his knife sticking out of the fire pit. I strain to reach it before him, but the pain in my leg pins me in place. And I've neither the strength nor courage to fight it. Had I the great knife, what would I do with it anyway?

More importantly, what will he?

CHAPTER 35

Hilt in hand, the crazed man raises the blade to his face and blows on the smoking tip. Its orange glow flickers in his dark eyes. He grunts, satisfied, and kneels beside me, gripping the knee of my injured leg. I try to squirm free, for whatever he's got planned, it can't be good, but his scarred fingers hold me with all the strength of his metal traps. He slips the smoldering blade under the scarf I'd tied as a bandage and with a quick jerk slices it off. The edges of the wool melt and ignite as it falls free. With his razor-hot edge, he cuts along what's left of my trouser leg, and bares my leg to the firelight. The wounds are worse than I thought, for three livid gashes pierce my leg and four others pulse on the underside. My pounding heart gushes new blood through unbound punctures, spilling it in puddles on the dirt floor. I'll surely die from them if they're not seen to, but, right now, the madman with the knife seems more fatal.

What is he going to do? Is he going to kill me? To cut me into chunks for trap bait?

My heart drums in my ears. "Don't ..." I whimper. "Please."

But he avoids my eyes, the same way I do with any prey, as he lowers the fiery blade to my bare skin. The pain is unbearable. It sears through my leg, indeed through my whole body, as I clench and scream, writhing on the dirt floor. The white pain seems to last forever, but moments later it ebbs to a red hot pulse.

My leg. My leg. He has surely cut it off.

I don't want to look, but I have to see. I have to know. As he turns to put the knife blade back in the fire, I swallow and look down my trembling body. I'm whole. I blink and shift my head to the side for a better look. Sure enough, my leg is still there, still a bloody mess, except for the largest puncture just above my knee. Blackened blood surrounds a crimson shape, a smear of scalded skin three inches wide. I know then what he wants, the truth of it drifting to me on the smoke of my singed skin, for the burn mark is a triangle the exact size and shape of his knife's tip. The exact size and shape of the burns on his forearm.

Branded.

He wipes his melting face with the back of his scarred hand, then picks up the knife and turns me. I won't let him torture me like this, even if it kills me. I'll die fighting, so I will. Before he grabs my bare knee, I kick him hard with my good leg drawing on whatever dregs of strength I've left. It catches him by surprise and knocks him back into the fire pit. His howl fills the tiny shack and I know he's burned, but I don't wait to find out how badly. Rolling to my stomach, I push to my knees and try to rise. The doorway. Freedom waits just a few steps away. But I can't stand, much less step. My right leg gives and I cry out as I collapse to the ground. I'll have to crawl out. Heaving my body across the dirt floor, I push with my arms and my left leg, flopping like a fish, but it moves me forward until my fingers graze the door's wood. I know another two or three good shoves will free me. But I never get the chance to find out.

A hand yanks the scruff of my shirt and drags me back. I fight with all my soul, but no matter how I flail, I'm no match for him. He tosses me beside the fire and grips the knife once more.

"Don't," I beg, for 'tis all I've left in me to do. The tears come then, for I know all is lost. I sob in great heaving breaths, exhausted from the fight. From all the trials that led me to this cursed place.

"I have to." His voice is thick. "It's for your own good."

"Please ... please ... don't burn me."

He hesitates, looks at the skull wall, and finally turns his dark eyes to mine. Be it the fire's glow or my own desperation playing tricks, for a moment, as we hold each other's gaze, I'm sure 'tis sympathy I see. But not for long.

Instead, I see his teeth grit; I see the hilt in his thick fist bearing down on my head and, with a sickening crack, darkness spills out and I see no more.

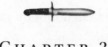

CHAPTER 36

The next few hours are just a sweltering blur. I slip in and out of consciousness, unsure which one is the real nightmare. Images flicker before my eyes. The red-hot blade. Watchful skulls. But always I see that twisted face. Its grotesque grimace is seared into my brain. My head throbs and my thigh screams as though the blade is there, scorching still. I don't know where I am, why he's captured me, or who this crazy animal skinner is—all I know for sure is that I'm injured, captive, and sweltering. This must surely be hell.

I moan and raise a hand to rub my forehead, surprised to find a hard lump. *He hit me.* I try to rise but the room spins and I lie back down, though not before glancing at my leg. Each puncture wound is a red-raw burn in the shape of his knife tip. They weep and blister, rimmed in blackened skin and crusted blood. *He burned me.* But I'm surprised at the feeling of relief. *He didn't kill me.* Not yet, anyway.

I glance around the small shack. There's no sign of him. A cup of water and a few strips of dried meat sit next to me. I should try and escape while he is gone—but I know I haven't the strength. It takes me all I have to get up on one elbow and bring the cup to my parched mouth. I can almost hear the hiss of the water as it hits my lips.

"You are awake." His raspy voice makes me drop the cup and spill what's left. "You slept for days," he adds, entering the shack, carrying a great hoop stretching some kind of animal skin.

Days?

"Yes, yes. I know," he whispers at the skulls on the wall. "Quiet! Let me talk to him."

"You burned my leg," I say. It's meant to sound like an accusation, but it comes out more like a whimpering question.

He clenches his jaw. "Had to." Sitting on the other side of the fire, he begins to undo the lacing, pulling the hide taut across the sapling frame. "They said there was no other way." He rocks slightly as he speaks. "Had to."

The man is clearly mad. And I'll not be hanging around, waiting for them skulls to tell him it's time to do me in.

"I need to go now," I say, "back to the shanty." I speak slowly, clearly, as though talking to a young child. "They'll be looking for me."

Truth be told, I'll bet no one is looking for me, but he

doesn't know that. I'll bet he doesn't know anything.

"Away," he says, pulling the rope through as he rips the stitches with his twisted fingers. "Logs are on the river." He nods as he rocks. "Only me, now." He stops then and looks at me with that frozen smile. "And you. Me and you."

My gut is screaming to get out of here, but the pain screaming in my leg is much louder. A few more days, that's all I need, and I'll be strong enough to escape. If he wanted to kill me, he'd have already done it. Right? But somehow that doesn't make me feel any better.

He finishes with the unlacing and tosses the frame aside, before laying the skin on the ground, fur side up. Despite the heat, a cold shiver ripples up my back. I'd know that fur anywhere—black-tipped and creamy.

No!

I can't speak.

He strokes the fur with his mutilated hands, picks it up, and flicks it like a rug before rolling it and piling it on the great mound of animal skins in the corner. He must have forty or fifty, at least. But all I can think of is the last one on the top. I can't take my eyes off it.

"What—is that ...?" There isn't enough air in this tiny shack. " Is it ...?"

Then he turns back to me with the answer on his scarred lips.

Don't say it! Don't say it!

But through the puckered mask he rasps one word, wet and dreadful. "Wolf."

CHAPTER 37

Today is the day. I'm breaking out. I've watched this Skinner's habits; I know his routine. He's going to check the traps today. He'll be gone the better part of the morning and when he is, I'm grabbing my knife and getting the hell out of this godforsaken place.

Skinner. That's what I call him. For that's all he is. All he does. He's consumed with his furs and traps. Hoarding his pelts in his darkened corner, hides he's stolen from the Wawaties. 'Twas him Mahingan saw pilfering the foxes. I'm sure of it. Each night Skinner sits in the dark corner, counting and stroking all his furs as he mutters to himself. He's skinned every kind of animal. Well, almost every kind. One remains. So he talks to the skulls about his plans to get it. To put its skull in the empty spot on the wall. At first, I thought he was talking about me—but 'tis the bear he's after. Still, my skull won't feel safe until it's resting on my shanty bunk, or better yet, in my bed back home. Wherever that may be.

My leg isn't healed. Far from it. But I've been practicing walking on it. Every day when he leaves, I get up and stagger about the small room for hours. It kills me, so it does, and I can't put much weight on it for long, but one of the Y-sticks used for the spit over the fire makes a fair crutch. There's no way I can outrun him, but with a few hours head start and a good snowfall like there is now, to cover my tracks, I may just make it. I have to.

I keep my eyes shut in the morning, pretend to sleep. Sure enough, after he eats his porridge, and straps on his blades and gear, I hear him leave. As soon as the door shuts, I hop over, open it a crack, and watch him tromp into the woods. I wait a few more minutes despite the sharp draft cutting through the gap. I want to be sure he's good and gone.

Now's my chance!

I tie a strip of hide around the leg of my breeches where the trap and trapper had ripped them asunder. Boots and coat on, I limp to his wall of weapons and take my knife back. I'm half tempted to take one of his bigger knives just to have it for protection, but God knows what he's killed with it. I don't want those dirty blades anywhere near me.

Propping the Y-stick under my arm, I hobble out the door, blinking blindly like a mole in the sun. After so many hours in that dingy shack, the snow's brightness is like two thumbs pushing against my eyeballs, making them ache and water. But that's the least of my worries. Which way is the shanty? Or the river? Even if I found the river, this leg'll surely not get me very far. I daresay any town is a good hike from here. Unsure of where to go, I head in the opposite direction of Skinner's tracks. As far away from him as I can get, is a good place to start.

Hours later, I stop and settle on a fallen log. It's been slow going, much slower than I thought. I glance behind but, thankfully, there's no sign of Skinner. Rolling my shoulder eases the muscle spasm, yet does nothing for the burn in my armpit where the blasted crutch has rubbed me raw. But it's my leg that's giving me the most pain. Every burnt puncture beats with my heart, throbbing louder and louder as I grow weaker. If the shanty isn't over that next hill, I'll have to use what strength I've left to build a lean-to for the night. I should have taken back my flint. At least then I'd have a fire. I curse myself for not thinking ahead.

I don't even hear him coming, which is surprising, given his ragged breath. He looms over me, hands on his hips, three rabbits hanging stiffly from his belt. Skinner.

"There you are!" he yells.

I turn and bolt but, after three or four stumbling steps, he's got me by the scruff. He says nothing as he trudges back to the shack, my collar in one fist and the Y-stick in the other. At first I kick and wriggle, but I haven't the strength to fight him. And so I hang there, feet dragging in the snow. As helpless as the stiff rabbits.

When we reach the shack, he throws me inside and storms out, only to return moments later with a trap and mallet. Muttering to himself, he holds the spike at the end of the short chain and drives it deep in the ground. Buried in solid rock, that spike is never coming out. I'm terrified that he's going to shut that trap's mouth around my good leg, but he removes the trap from the chain, leaving a shackle of sorts, which he brusquely closes around my ankle.

"Just let me go," I whimper, "please."

He clenches his jaw as he screws the bolt, clamping the manacle tight.

"Why are you doing this to me?" The unfairness of it all overwhelms me. Lost, confused, abandoned. And now, this. "You can't just kidnap some stranger and—"

"Stranger?" he stops and turns to me. Sweat glistens on the ripples of his marred skin. He puts his disfigured hand on my arm. Its touch makes my skin crawl. "Don't you remember?"

I don't know what he's on about. As much as I'd like to, I know I'd never forget a face like his. All I know is he's crazy. Insane.

"Do you remember anything ... your home, your mother, the house fire ... Owen?" he says, his eyes boring into mine.

"Owen?" The name is odd on my tongue. "I don't know any Owen or—"

"That's your name." His words fall upon me. "*You're* Owen."

What?

All this time, I've wanted answers, though now I'm not so sure. I rub my forehead as I stare into the fire. I have to ask. I have to know. "Do you ... do you know me?" I say, afraid that he might.

"Know you?" He grabs my arms in his hands. Shakes me slightly. "Owen, it's me, son. Your father."

CHAPTER 38

I can't believe it. I won't. This man isn't my father.

Is he?

I lie down where I'm chained. Stare into the fire. Everything in my being tells me it's not true. But maybe I just don't want it to be true. He says he's chaining me up because this isn't the first time I've run away from him. Surely, he's insane.

Or maybe I am.

I don't want to believe him, but when he said our house burned down, I saw it. I saw it in my mind's eye as clear as the flames in the fire pit before me. Men riding into my yard. Torches tossed on the roof. I remember it. The crackle of thatch igniting, the whoosh of fire swallowing my home. I can almost feel the smoke stinging my eyes and burning in my lungs. I remember filling a bucket from the rain barrel and tossing it at a fire that needed a hundred more to stop it. And I remember the men pulling on the crossbeams, trying to tumble the flaming roof. I ran at them, pulled at their arms. But I was too small. With one slap they sent me reeling. After that, I remember no more.

Was Skinner there? Is that how he got his burn scars?

I can't say for sure. But I know the father from my dreams—he wasn't there during the fire. I look at Skinner where he sits, sharpening his great blade. Maybe the father of my dreams is only that. The father I created to make up for the man before me. Maybe I can't remember my family because I wanted to forget about Skinner. Wanted to forget I ever knew him. Wanted to forget the very blood that runs in my veins.

I shudder at the possibility. I don't know who Owen is or was. But he's not me. Dear God in heaven, I hope he's not me.

Though I've stopped notching them, the days roll on. Skinner—for I'll not call him father no matter how often he asks, not in a million years—has lengthened my chain so I can work outside. I've crudely stitched my pant leg and the leg inside it is near healed. Strong, but forever scarred. *Like Skinner,* I think and push the thoughts away. *No, I'm nothing like him.*

I clean all the bloodied skins he lugs home, string them up on great hoops, and scrape away what flesh remains on the inside; steep them in the liquid Skinner makes of oak leaves, bark, and acorns; stretch and hang them to dry. 'Tis messy work, and hard, too. My back and arms ache by the day's end. And when I close my eyes, all I see are scraped skins, husks of animals that used to be. I'm one myself. Trapped, scarred, and empty. I have stopped trying to remember anything more. I don't want to know where I came from. 'Tis hard enough dealing with where I am.

But in those moments before I wake, a fierce longing rushes over me like the tide. Green meadows. Rolling hills. A white stone cottage with yellow thatch. I let myself go there, sometimes, to that place of dreaming. And I see that man. The one I so wished were real. We're walking the country road. Fishing. Fetching kelp for the potato beds. Playing the whistle together.

Skinner's wet snores from the corner seep into the dream and I roll over, cover my ears. I'm there now. *Home ... with Da*. Even if it is a fantasy.

"Watch me, Da! I taught Squib how to show jump." Da stops his shoveling and leans over the stone wall for a better look. Wait 'til he sees this. I pound the sides of the donkey's barrel belly with my bare feet and he bolts. We've done it a thousand times this morning, or twice, at least. But as Squib approaches the one-foot fence I've built, he balks and kicks up both back legs. With a yelp, off I go, flying over rein and rail, landing face first in a pile of muck. The dark-haired girl

is laughing at me again. I hate it when she does that. I'm sulking, so I am, my head in a black thundercloud.

Da comes over and hands me his hankie. He grabs the rope harness and strokes Squib's nose as I wipe my face. "So what say you, Squib? Which of you's more stubborn?" He tousles my hair and laughs. His smile is brilliant, like the sun coming out. "I daresay there's none more willful and determined than my boy."

And I want to believe him. To believe in him. Dear God in heaven, how I want to.

CHAPTER 39

"They'll be watching you," Skinner says, nodding at the skulls. I don't know if he means it as a threat or encouragement. Either way, as small as the shack is, I've been doing my best to ignore that wall.

He's going to track the bear. Won't be back for a few days. What do I care? I'm just glad I won't have to listen to his phlegmy snore all night. I might even open the door and air out the place.

He checks my chain and shackle. Pounds the spike two more times with his mallet just to be sure. "Finish the rabbit hides. I'm bringing back the bear," he says, eyes glittering. "The weather is changing. I bet it's waking."

I look away. *Just go.*

After he leaves, I do my chores. Chop more wood. Build two stretching frames. Scrape the rabbit skins. With him gone, I have some freedom. I snort. *Freedom? Well, as far as this chain will reach.* He's right, though. The weather is changing. I smell it in the wet air. A hint of spring. It makes going back into that foul-smelling cabin even worse. It must be the hides in the corner. I decide to air them out. Maybe a few hours hanging on the line will get rid of some of that stink. I don't remember the Wawaties' hides smelling anything like this.

I carry them out by the armloads and drape them over the line, over branches and tree limbs. But it's only when I get to the last one that I find the box. A small chest about a foot long. I sniff it, afraid this is the source of the bad smell. God knows what he's got in here. But there's no scent when I open it. Inside, I find a curled scrap of newspaper and a framed portrait, singed and sooty around the edges. It's a pencil sketch, a rather good one, of a man with a thick handlebar mustache, standing with his hand on the shoulder of a light-haired boy about nine years old. In the bottom corner of the sketch is one word: *Lilian.* The artist's name, perhaps. I open the yellowed newspaper. Some words are hard to make out, for I'm not so good with letters, but I get the gist just the same.

Bytown Gazette — July 12, 1845

Fire on George Street.

Fire broke out at the home of Mr. William Slattery, the local butcher, Friday night. Though the fire brigade arrived and neighbors fetched Mr. Slattery from Burpee's Tavern, the fire quickly spread and raged out of control. Despite Fire Chief Patterson's protests that the building was not safe, Mr. Slattery ran into the flaming home to save his wife and son. Slattery suffered life-threatening burns to most of his body and is convalescing under the care of Dr. Van Cortlandt. A funeral mass will be said at Notre Dame Cathedral on Monday at two o'clock for the repose of the souls of Mr. Slattery's wife Lilian and their nine-year-old son Owen.

Owen?

I'm not Owen. I look at the portrait again. At the man's eyes so clearly captured in a few lead strokes. *But that is Skinner.*

Sure enough, it's him. Not the broken and twisted man Skinner is, but the strapping husband and father William was.

So, I'm not his son.

The news brings me some relief but, strangely, I also feel pity for Skinner. He'd gotten those scars trying to save his family. He'd lost his wife and child. I can only imagine the guilt he must feel for not being able to save them. Enough to make him crazy, no doubt.

I read the article again. *Local butcher.* That explains his knives. Still, he burned me with them ... branded me ... But I have to admit, my leg has healed strong and true. After a gashing by those dirty trap teeth, I might have lost my leg altogether. Maybe he'd fixed my wounds like he did his own, the only way he knew how—he'd cauterized them. Burned them closed.

None of this excuses what he's done to me—especially this shackling—but it helps me make some sense of it. If he thinks I am really Owen, losing me again must terrify him. Which means he will do anything to keep me.

And that terrifies me all the more.

My mind races the rest of the day, trying to figure a way to escape. I pull on the chain until my hands are red raw, but that spike won't budge.

It's only later that night, as I lie by the glowing fire and let my mind slip back to the white thatched cottage that I feel hope sprout. 'Tis no fantasy. They're memories. That man, my real da, the one in my dreams, he truly exists!

And I'm going to get out of here and find him.

CHAPTER 40

I'm up before the sun, draping my chain in the bed of embers. *Why didn't I think of this before?* If the smith at the loggers' shanty can heat iron so it bends into a horse's shoe, surely I can heat these links enough to break them apart.

It takes much longer than I thought for the metal to redden enough. But when it's glowing, I prop the links on a flat fireplace stone and, using a smaller rock, bash the chain. Sparks fly off with every strike and the metal cools very quickly. I have to keep firing it after every second or third strike, but the links are thinning, I swear it.

Sure enough, after a few more hits, the chain snaps. *I'm free!*

I take my knife. My flint. A bit of food. I won't be caught again. Not this time. I plan on running until nightfall.

The weather is milder and the sun is shining. A good sign.

I can make some ground in these conditions. All the physical labor these past two weeks has made me stronger, and I decide to head for the river. All or nothing. Even if I found the shanty, that would be the first place Skinner would look for me. It makes no sense to go back there. I set out at a good clip, despite the manacle still weighing on my ankle. None of that matters now. I'm free. Free!

After a few hours, I stop to eat some of the dried meat strips I'd packed and take a drink of snow melted in my hands. Red berries on a nearby bush catch my eye and I pick a few. They have no smell. I wonder if I can eat them. I check the other side for more.

"Owen?" a voice yells.

It can't be. It can't. But I turn to see Skinner, standing about fifty feet away. He seems surprised to see me. But no more surprised than I am, for the madman stands, gun at the ready. He closes one eye and sights along the barrel. This time he's not taking me home. This time he's going to kill me.

"Don't shoot!" I plead. "Don't!"

He's going to do it; he's going to pull the trigger. But just as I think he will, a flash of fur streaks from the left, hitting Skinner's arm and knocking the barrel. His shot erupts in a puff of smoke and the gun drops from his hands, but I don't have time to worry about Skinner or what hit him, as the bush behind me explodes with a thundering roar. *A bear!* 'Tis near two hundred pounds of angry muscle and empty stomach, only five feet away from me. Its bloodied muzzle, grazed by Skinner's bullet, slathers as it tosses its head. Its massive paws swat at the ground, raking long lines with its hooked claws. It's ready to attack, but I can't move. Terror shackles me to the spot.

The bear lunges for me and with one swipe of its thick arm, sends me to the ground, hard. Be the air knocked or shocked from me, either way, I can't breathe, as I look up and see the animal looming, paw raised, ready for the killing strike.

Will it rip me from gizzard to gullet? Crush me? Maul me?

"OWEN—NO!" The guttural cry interrupts the bear and it turns its attention on Skinner, rising to its hind legs to meet him as he rushes it, knives in both his hands. They fight, tooth and blade, tearing into one another. Hot blood splatters on the snow, on me. I can't watch and yet, I can't rip my eyes away.

Something grabs my collar and drags me from the fight.

Wolf? Wolf!

I haven't the breath to speak his name. Can't believe he's here. Alive.

Skinner falls and the bear pounces upon him, pounding him beneath its wide paws until Skinner stops moving. Enraged and wounded by Skinner's knives, the bear turns to face us. I drag myself to my feet as the wolf moves between me and the bear. As brave as he is, fur bristled, fangs bared, the wolf is no match for this bear. And I'm in no shape to run. We're done for, surely done for.

A searing pain pierces my shoulder, and shoves me forward, sending me to my knees just as the bear makes his move. *Thunk!* An arrow appears in the bear's chest. Then another. And another. I look back to the woods from where they came—to see Mahingan Wawatie emerging from the tree line, lowering his bow. The bear staggers and falls in the snow, breathing its last.

"You killed it ..." I gasp. "You killed the bear."

Mahingan stands over it, his hands shaking slightly, a hint of shock on his face. I can only imagine the look on mine.

"You ... you shot me ..." In the corner of my eye, I can just make out the feathered shaft sticking out of my back. The arrowhead sears inside my shoulder, as my body tries to throb it out. My head swoons.

A gurgle comes from Skinner and I crawl over to his side. His face is even more distorted from the bear's attack and blood spurts from the bite in his neck. A fatal wound. There's no saving him, not now.

"Owen ..." he says, choking. He raises his mangled fingers. And I know one thing I can do for him.

I take his hand in mine. "I'm here."

His eyes search for me, focus on me for a second. He's not

long in this world.

"You did it—" I say, clutching his hand, "you saved me ... Father."

He weakly squeezes my hand and then lets go—of the guilt, of the pain, of the last breath of life.

CHAPTER 41

The agony wakens me and I find myself lying on my side in the snow next to Skinner. Grandfather Wawatie kneels by my head, gripping the arrow still stuck in my back. He grunts and something snaps. Even though I see the broken, feathered shaft he tosses in the snow, the pain shooting through my shoulder has me convinced he's broken my collar bone.

"Here," he puts a leather strap in between my teeth. "Bite down. This might hurt."

Might hurt?!

He rests one hand on the front of my shoulder and with the other grips the stub of shaft. But instead of pulling it out, Grandfather Wawatie drives it deeper. The arrow head rips through my flesh and, no matter how I arch in agony and clench my jaw, I can't stop the pain.

What the hell is he doing? Pull it out. Out! Not in!

With two strong thrusts, the tip pierces through the front of my chest just under my collar bone, and Grandfather's strong fingers pull it free. My shoulder throbs and burns and my face is covered in sweat. I want to pass out. To throw up. To curse Grandfather for driving it deeper and punch Mahingan for hitting me in the first place.

"You did well," the old man says.

Mahingan takes it and wipes the head in the snow, cleaning it of my blood.

"Am I—" I swallow, as Grandfather presses snow against the wound. "Am I going to die?" My voice is raspy. I don't want to hear the answer, but I have to know.

"Yes," Mahingan answers.

"But not today," his grandfather adds. "The wound is clean."

He could have fooled me. It felt like he was up to his bloody elbows in my shoulder.

Grandfather binds the wound. I wait for Mahingan to be chastised—after all, the boy did try to kill me—but the old man says nothing.

"You shot me." I say again as I sit up. "I can't believe it. You actually shot me."

He doesn't even apologize. He seems proud of it. Then I'm left to sulk and suffer while they turn their attention to the bear. After a prayer of thanks, Mahingan tosses some of the steaming entrails to the wolf and his own dog. The wolf takes it with him into the woods.

"How did you know where I was?" I finally ask when my heart slows to a regular beat.

"The Wolf told us," Mahingan says, not looking up as he helps his grandfather skin the bear. "We were way out on our trapline and it kept appearing. Day after day. *Mishomis* said it wanted us to follow. And so we did. But when it started running today, *Mishomis* told me to keep up with it. After all, I *am* the fastest runner. Then I heard the gun and the bear."

They cut up the meat, wrapping it in smaller packages and loading it on Grandfather Wawatie's sled beside the bear hide. During the hour or so it takes them to prepare the skin, meat, and bones, I collect a few rocks with my good arm and pile them in a cairn over Skinner's body. I'm thankful for the Wawaties' help, for my shoulder is throbbing and I haven't the strength to cover his whole body. Using my knife, I carve *William Slattery* on a bit of wood and leave it on the mound. It isn't much, but it's something. It's near dark by the time our work is done.

"Come to our camp," Grandfather Wawatie says as he picks up the sled rope. "We will tend your shoulder. And celebrate Mahingan's kill."

I look at Mahingan, unsure if he wants me there, but he's bursting with pride. "I killed a bear!"

"Skinner's knives helped," I mutter.

"I brought down a bear with three shots," he grins at me. "And a *shognosh* with one," he adds, outside his grandfather's hearing.

I can't stand that boy. Had I any other option, I'd be going as far from him as I could. He tried to kill me, I'm sure of it. And I'll bet he'll try again.

CHAPTER 42

We trudge through the woods for what seems like hours, before arriving at their camp by the river. Only, unlike their small trapline camp, this one has three large bark-covered shelters, upturned canoes, several skinned carcasses smoking over fires, and numerous hides hanging on stretching frames. Mahingan's family gathers to meet us. Grandfather Wawatie introduces me and speaks to them in their language. I don't catch their names, but I nod politely at Mahingan's mother and sisters, his uncles, aunts, and cousins of all ages. I've never met his father, and yet, even I feel his absence. Like the open glade of a felled tree. The sense that something solid and strong once stood here. I see Mahingan looking beyond his uncles as though he feels it, too.

A small hand tugs on mine and I look down at Mahingan's

youngest sister. "Chiki," she announces, pointing at herself. Her earnestness, despite her missing two front teeth, makes me smile.

One of the men, a son of Grandfather Wawatie, it seems, speaks lowly and gestures at their hunting sled. It seems they had less success at their traps, for their mound of fur and packaged meat is nearly half of what Grandfather and Mahingan brought.

Grandfather Wawatie waves his hand as if to say this is not the time to speak of it. Instead, he claps Mahingan's shoulder and gestures at the bear meat weighing down their sled.

A taller boy pats Mahingan on the back. Even in the dim light, Mahingan's smile shines like a crescent moon.

The women scurry around and, in minutes, have cleared the sleds of all meat and fur. Even before we have put away the sled and snowshoes, smells of cooking bear meat waft from the cabin. The space inside is warm and inviting, from its spruce-lined floor to the moss-chinked walls. A fire burns at the center where the women and girls work, stirring pots that hang from wooden crossbars. Dough-capped sticks stand propped over the flame, each being carefully rotated by Chiki. After Mahingan's mother checks my shoulder, she boils the bark she's stripped off a birch sapling and applies it to my wound as a poultice. Then she invites me to sit in the corner next to the bundles and baskets. It seems every person but me has a job to do. After so long in Skinner's dismal shack, I'm happy just to be here in the midst of family bustle and banter, even if they speak to each other in words I don't understand. I slip off my belt and start to carve a bear paw at the end opposite the wolf print. A great oval with five small circles spreading over the top, each ending with a clawed tip.

The bundled package next to me begins to wail and, as I peek around the wood frame propped against the wall, I realize 'tis no parcel, but a baby. I'm so surprised by it, I do nothing but stare at its wee face, scrunched and bright red, as the screaming continues. Tears spring from its eyes as its tiny tongue trembles with its howling.

"Like this," Chiki says, squatting beside me. She stands the board up and moves it side to side. Sure enough, the babe quiets. "You take care of your brothers or sisters, too, right?"

I don't know how to answer her. Did I?

"Your English is good," I say, instead.

"*Mishomis* teaches me. He says it is good to speak the language for trading."

Perhaps my family is one of those that trade with the Wawaties. If nothing else, the Wawaties might know of my da, but before I can ask, Chiki's mother calls and points at the fire.

"The bannock!" Chiki rushes back to salvage the smoldering food. The minute she turns, the baby lets out another wail—only this time, there's no one but me to help him. I do as Chiki instructed and, sure enough, the crying stops.

Soon, the women have the meal prepared. We sit on the spruce-covered floor in a circle around the steaming bowls of meat and soups, baskets of dried berries, hot cedar tea, and a heaping pile of Chiki's bannock. Just like the meal in the trapline *pikogan*, Grandfather fills a plate from each bowl and, praying, scrapes it into the fire. This time he dips his hands in the bear grease and wipes it through his hair and then invites Mahingan to do the same. I don't know the meaning of it—but I can tell by Mahingan's reaction 'tis a great honor.

Then we eat. 'Tis surely a feast, for I'm near bursting by the time we're done. Mahingan hands me a burnt piece of bannock. I don't think I can eat another bite, but Chiki's wide eyes beside me are waiting. Mahingan elbows his cousin and the pair start to laugh as I bite into the charred bread.

"Chiki," I say, through blackened lips. "I do believe this is the best bannock I've ever tasted!"

She claps her hands and breaks into a gap-toothed grin.

Wreathed in pipe smoke, the men tell stories well into the night. First Grandfather Wawatie, then his sons Kijick and Matawa, and finally their sons, share tales of the hunt. I don't know the words—but their lively actions and excited voices tell it well enough. The little ones have already drifted off by the time their parents carry them to their blankets and furs where the family will sleep.

In a space of my own, lying on my good shoulder, I settle in for the night, wrapped in the rabbit-fur blanket Mahingan's mother provided. Grandfather Wawatie sits by the fire, beating a drum, soft, then strong. *Ba-boom. Ba-boom. Ba-boom.* Like a heartbeat, lulling all to sleep. He starts to sing, then. In the melody of vowels melting, one into the other, I feel his story. The joy and loss. The yearning and hope. Foreign words with common heart.

With stories said and sung, soon everyone is silent. I hear their breathing grow long as each one sinks deeper into dreaming. But I can't sleep. I need to know my stories. My ancestors. I need to know it all. For what good is a man with no story?

CHAPTER 43

I'm soaked to the skin, heedless to the chill of that Feb-
ruary rain, as I run up the muddy road that night. Da
should have been back by now. Mick and him always
*arrived home in the dark after their long day's labor on the
Road Works, but not this late. Something is wrong.*

I should be with them. *The thought, like a pebble long
dropped in my mind, ripples on and on. But the law only al-
lows one worker per family. And so I'd sit on that stone wall
outside that yellow-thatched cottage and watch Da leave every morning. And every evening, when he'd come down the
road that winds through the hills, there'd be less and less of
him. No matter how I begged Mam and Da, they wouldn't let
me take his place. You're too small, son, they said. You're not
able. And so Da went, day after day, trading his life for pen-
nies he never got paid.*

I know it before I see the wagon come over the hill, before I see the look on Mick's face. I know it before my sister cries out or my mother runs past me to the side of the wagon, reaching in to take Da's hand. To try and hold him here with us.

He's gone, I just know it. My da is dead.

I can't move. Can't breathe. I should have been there. I should have been there.

The boulders he bore, hour after hour, building those roads, eventually wore him down. Mam and Da, they thought I was too weak, too small—but I now bear the heaviest burden. It weighs upon my shoulders and crushes my heart.

I should have been there. This is all my fault.

"Da!" I scream, bolting from my deep sleep. In the darkness, a baby cries. Muffled voices grumble.

I can't breathe ... I can't breathe. Tossing the blanket, I stumble for the doorway, heedless of how many people I've trodden across. *Outside ... outside ... I need air!*

Bursting through the doorway, I fall into the snow, landing on my hands and knees, drawing great heaving breaths as though each was my last. They turn to sobs, gut-wrenching hurls of tears and snot. *Da ... Da ... he's not looking for me ... he's not coming for me ...* 'Tis as though I've just lost him this moment. I suppose, in a way, I have.

A hand rests on my shoulder. I know without looking it's Grandfather Wawatie. He doesn't sit down by me. He doesn't lift me up. He just stands by, waiting with me, while I ride out this storm. I suppose there is nothing he could have said or done. Nothing will bring Da back. But somehow it helps to know I am not alone. I wipe my runny nose on my sleeve and sit back on my haunches, shuddering now and then in the wake of the outburst.

"My father ..." I say, hoarsely. "He ... he is dead."

Saying makes it real, and I moan as the undertow of sadness draws me back, washes over me.

Grandfather drapes his blanket across my shoulders. He slips back into the shelter and I cry at the moon until the sun rises.

CHAPTER 44

"What exactly are we looking for?" I ask Mahingan as we search the forest. I've been avoiding him the past few days. Avoiding all of them. My shoulder is healing well, but my father's death is like an aching hole deep inside me. It festers and stings and there's no medicine for it. That wound will never heal, for Da's not coming for me. Ever. Nothing else matters.

Mahingan circles around the trunks, looking for something. He's annoyed that his grandfather insisted he take me with him.

"I can't help you if I don't know what we need to find," I say. I don't want to be here, either.

Mahingan clenches his jaw and continues his search, stopping every now and then to pick up a small boulder which, after inspecting, he tosses aside. Finally, he finds one.

"You want to help? Carry this." He dumps it into my hands. 'Tis only a plain gray rock about the size of my head. When we find two more that meet his standards, we trek back to see Grandfather Wawatie. He appraises the stones and decides only one is worth keeping, before sending us back into the bush to find even more.

"What's so special about them?" I ask, holding up the next stone he's given me. Again, 'tis nothing but a rock. Mahingan ignores me. "Aren't they just plain old stones?"

Mahingan finally stops and turns toward me. "See? That's exactly what I mean. I can't believe he's inviting you to the sweat. You don't even know what you are holding."

I take another look. "It's a rock."

"It's a *grandfather,*" Mahingan says, exasperated.

"Your grandfather is a *rock?*" I've heard of shape-shifting, but this is something new.

Mahingan shakes his head. "No, *shognosh.* You don't understand our ways. None of you do."

"Well, then, explain it to me," I say. "You can't be angry with me for not knowing what I've never learned."

He puts his hand on the rock in mine. "This has been part of our Earth Mother since ... forever." He waves his other hand, taking in the woods around us. "Before the *Anishnaabeg,* before animals, before any plant or trees, rocks—the mountains—have always been. They have been here the longest. That's why they're called grandfathers. They're wise ancestors."

I have to think about it for a while, but it makes sense.

In a way.

"Never mind," Mahingan says, turning back to his search.

"So ..." I study this ancient stone more carefully. "So then, this is *my* grandfather, too."

Mahingan considers my comment. The jut of his jaw tells me he's not happy, but his silence tells me I'm right.

Grandfather Wawatie has rejected double what he kept but, eventually, he seems happy enough with the stones we've found. He gives them to Kijick, and I wonder what they're going to do with them. I don't have to wonder long, though. A few hours later, at Grandfather's word, his sons and grandsons head into the woods. Unsure, I stand and watch them leave. Grandfather Wawatie stops beside me and nods. I think he wants me to follow him. And so I do.

Not far from the main camp is a squat, domed structure, covered in animal skins. A flap hangs over a low door at the front. Grandfather leads us just in front of the dome to where Kijick tends the fire. All twelve rocks Mahingan and I collected are being heated in the flames. Kijick hands Grandfather Wawatie a small bowl and a feather. The dried grass inside the bowl smolders. It smells of cedar, sage maybe, and something else sweet and strong. Smoke drifts up around Grandfather Wawatie's face like incense, and, with a feather, he waves it over each of his sons and grandsons with all the reverence of a bishop and his censer. He comes to me then and does the same. I copy what the others have done, cupping the smoke in my hands and pouring it over my face, my heart, and down my legs.

The men and boys strip down to nothing. And though I hesitate at first—it is winter, after all—I copy the others. Taking a pinch of tobacco, each person sprinkles it on the fire before saying their name and crawling into the lodge. It reminds me of Grandfather Wawatie's food offering. Mahingan and I are the last in line. Numb, I am, with the cold from standing stark naked in a forest in the dead of winter. I half want to put my coat back on while I wait, but if Mahingan can stand it, well then, so can I. Still, when it's my turn, I want to throw the tobacco and hurry inside, but I remember what Grandfather said about the food offering. It's a way to say thanks and give honor. So I stop and think about how long the rocks have lasted—how short our time is. I think of Da and say a prayer for him as I sprinkle the tobacco.

I'm the last one to crawl into the lodge and so bloody cold I can hardly feel my hands and feet. The room is pitch black and I bump into a few others before finding the empty spot in the circle.

"Who are you?" Grandfather's bodiless voice asks. I'd forgotten that stating your name was part of entering the lodge.

Unsure of how to answer, I tell the truth. "I don't know, but I want to remember."

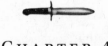

CHAPTER 45

Grandfather Wawatie calls and Kijick brings in one of the hot stones pinched between two carrying logs. It pulsates like a red heart, as it throws heat and light on the shadows of men and boys. Placing it in the middle of the lodge, Grandfather pours water on it, making it hiss and steam. Faces disappear in the mist. 'Tis as though I'm completely alone in this darkness. Grandfather sings a few songs, prayers, I think. Then he calls for Kijick to bring another rock. By the second or third stone, I'm warming up. By the tenth, I'm ready to pass out.

On Grandfather's word, everyone leaves the lodge. As I crawl out, I'm surprised to find them all lying in the snow. Naked or not, all I can think of is dousing my burning skin. I flop backwards into a drift and roll around. I don't know if it's the snow or myself that's melting—either way, I swear, I hear it hiss. Every part of my body is beating. I've never felt so alive. Just as the cool relief turns frigid, Grandfather calls us back inside the lodge, and the heat I once found unbearable wraps around me like a snug blanket.

After the next song, the lodge is a blister of steam. The very air itself scorches me. I can't breathe.

"Lie down," Grandfather suggests. "Put your face on the earth."

The dirt floor is cooler, but nothing stops the sweat pouring from every part of my body. It runs in rivulets down my face, my back, my chest. My hair is plastered to my head. My brain bubbles and throbs. Throbs. Throbs.

'Tis like the fever.

The memory emerges like tiny beads of sweat that gather together to saturate me.

I'm aboard the ship. The Dunbrody. *A soldier lifts Mam from the berth, where she's been lying in and out of consciousness for days. Take care of Annie, she'd said, her last words to me. And I did. I kept Annie away from the sickness on the ship, hiding out by the prow, telling her stories about the monk on the figurehead, the country that awaits us, the adventures ahead. And when we land at Grosse Isle quarantine station, and I feel the fever blazing behind my eyes, feel it banging in my brain and buckling my legs, I let the priests take her to the orphanage. I don't even say goodbye for fear she mightn't go.*

Kijick brings in the last two stones. At first, I don't know who he is. Sweat stings my eyes and I feel as though I've left my body.

Why shouldn't I? I'm all alone. I've no family. No one cares if I live or die. And I'm so tired, so very tired.

I don't know if I'm in a tent on Grosse Isle, or the Wawaties' lodge, or maybe hell itself.

Grandfather's face floats in and out of the steam. Voices sing in the darkness. Wolf's face appears as it did that night at the lean-to and, as I reach out to touch his fur, he raises his muzzle and joins the song ... hooOOOoooOoowl. I'm back on the island, lying among the sick and dying, and a girl's voice carries echoes in the distance ... *who-who-who* ... she's calling a name, my name, if I could only hear it ...

The men's song grows louder and louder in the lodge. Melting into the *who-who-who* beating in my head.

And then I see her entering the sick tent. Smaller, skinnier, ragged, and rough from the journey, my older sister, Kit. I thought we'd lost her back in Ireland. But she'd made it. She was alive! With every ounce of strength I have left, I push myself up and then she sees me. Runs to me. Wraps her arms around me. "I found you," she cries, squeezing me. "I found you, Jack."

JackByrne–JackByrne–JackByrne—my heart pounds the truth. It pulses through my veins and throbs in my very soul. I scramble for the door and rush into the night air. Emerging as slick and naked as a newborn, steam rises like incense from my sweating body as I stand and gaze at the great wide sky.

"Jack ..." I whisper at the net of stars. "I am Jack Byrne."

CHAPTER 46

The next day, life is very busy at the Wawatie camp. As well as their regular chores, the women are making baskets and whittling cedar spigots. Chiki tells me the maples are running. I look outside but they're still there. After my experience with the grandfathers in the sweat lodge, seeing a tree pick up and sprint over the hill isn't all that ridiculous.

"The sugar water, the *sap*, is running, Jack," Chiki explains.

I smile at the sound of my name. I love hearing it. I've even added it to my belt carvings just to see it boldly there.

She scrunches up her nose and looks at me. "Haven't you ever made maple syrup? Or *pigiwizigan?*"

"Taffy," her older sister Anami adds.

I shake my head. My inexperience, that so frustrates Mahingan, greatly fascinates his younger sister. I suppose with no one younger than her but the baby, Chiki loves having me as a student. And she's a better teacher than her older brother.

"Today's the perfect day," she says, piling the newly made birch-bark cups on the toboggan. I offer to pull it and she leads me and Anami into the woods. "The sap runs the best on sunny days like this, when there isn't much wind." Anami rolls her eyes at me as we follow behind Chiki, who chatters non-stop. For a wee thing, she sure knows a lot. "... And you have to make sure you don't tap too close to where you did last time, and put it on the white side of the tree, because the sap is better there."

Anami scouts the best trees, notching a small v in their trunks with her hatchet. I set the spigot in the v and Anami taps it in with hatchet's back end. After a few good thunks, the clear sap moves to the end of the spout and into the bark cup Chiki has hung beneath. Drip by drip by drip. I see now why Grandfather Wawatie teaches patience. Over the next few days, we tap a few more trees and go back to check our cups. We empty the sugar water into the large birch-bark basket on the back of the toboggan and lug it back to the clearing in the center, where Mahingan's mother and aunts boil the sap all day long over a great fire.

"How come you don't hunt with the boys?" Chiki asks me on a trek back.

"And risk getting accidentally shot in the back again?" I'm joking, sort of.

"That was no accident," Chiki says, her dark eyes serious. "Mahingan can hit a leaf bud from fifty feet away. He has a hawk's eye, him."

I frown. That hooligan did shoot me *on purpose*. I'd kind of hoped 'twas his aim that was off, not his character. But I should have known; the other three arrows hit within seconds and within inches of one another. He knew exactly what he was doing.

"Anyway, I didn't go with them because I wasn't invited." I say, thinking of Mahingan and his three cousins laughing at me that morning, as Chiki showed me how to wrap the bannock around the stick.

I don't know why he hates me so. He may be grieving, but so am I, truth be told. Maybe he's still angry about me being in the sweat lodge. Or maybe it's the knife. Grandfather Wawatie still has not given Mahingan his father's knife. Not even after the bear kill. I wonder what sort of feat Mahingan needs to do to get it. No doubt, Mahingan wonders that, too. Everyone else has been more than welcoming to me. But any fool can see he doesn't want me here at his camp.

Either way, it's clear he's sorry that he didn't kill me along with the bear.

CHAPTER 47

We take a moment to rest before moving on to the next grove of maples. I wipe my brow and rest against a trunk. The load is getting heavier with each stop. Chiki puts seeds in her bare hand and holds it up in the bright sun. Little black-capped birds flit past, settling in the branches above us. "Chicka-dee-dee-dee," Chiki sings, and the birds echo. One or two perch on the edge of her cupped palm, rewarded for their bravery with a few seeds.

"Thanks for helping us, Jack," Anami says.

"'Tis no bother at all. I'm happy to help out. My sister, Kit, and I often did the chores together back home in Ireland." It feels great to say it. To know it. To remember it all. And I do. Though some parts are painful to think on. "I haven't seen her in months. After our quarantine ended, she wanted me to come with her to Bytown to find our younger sister, Annie. But I had other plans. We had a huge fight, right there on the wharf. She was always telling me what to do, that Kit." I continue. "Ever since I can remember, she's been bossing me around. *Do this. Stop that. Stay here. Get that.*"

"Sounds like me and Mahingan," Anami says.

"Oh, but he *needs* to be told," I say, and we both laugh. "Still, Kit's only three years older than me, barely, and yet she acts like she's my mam. Well, that day, I told her she wasn't. I knew it hurt her. But still, I can't have her fussing over me like that, and I had great plans to go up the river and work the farms and lumber camps."

I pause for a moment, embarrassed at how those great plans had worked out.

"What did she say?" Anami asks.

"She just laughed at me like she always did. So I let her have it. *Where were you when Mam was sick?* I'd shouted at her. *When Annie cried? When Mam took her last breath? Who do you think took care of the family then, Kit? Not you. 'Twas me! I did!*"

I pause. "And what's worse, she *blamed* me. As though 'twas my fault Mam died and Annie was taken." My face burns at the thought of it. I'd done everything the best I could, but Kit always made me second-guess myself. I always had to prove myself to her and I was done with it. Done with her. "So I told her she didn't need to worry about me anymore. As far as I was concerned, she had no brother."

Why is it I can recall so clearly what I'd rather forget? I kick the snow at my feet. "That's the last time I saw her."

Anami's eyes hold no judgement. She knows all about brothers. Sure, isn't hers Mahingan Wawatie? The poor girl.

"You miss her," Chiki asks, brushing off her hand and slipping on her mitten, "your sister, Kit?"

"Yes."

"That is sad." Chiki tilts her head and looks at me for a moment. "You could go find her."

Chiki holds her idea out like a small seed. But I haven't the courage to take it. Kit wouldn't want to see me, anyway. Not after what I said to her at Grosse Isle. Not after what I did to Mick. I know Kit sent him to take care of me in the lumber camp. I know they loved each other—*begob*, I knew that before they did. No, I can't face her. Not after all the pain I've caused her.

"I bet she misses you, too," Anami adds. "Me, I miss Mahingan, when he's out on the traplines."

"Now, *that* is sad," I say. And the girls laugh.

CHAPTER 48

Chiki's mother drizzles hot, tawny syrup on the snow in three lines. Another thanksgiving prayer. Or so I thought.

"*Pigiwizigan!*" Chiki shrieks and kneels beside it, stripped twig in hand. The hardening syrup sticks to the tip of her stick and, with a few turns, Chiki swirls the gooey strip around the end. A great gob of glossy amber. She does the same with the other two strips and then hands them to Anami and me where we sit on the wide tree stump.

Copying the girls, I put mine on my tongue. 'Tis like I've died and gone to heaven. I've never tasted anything so sweet. Coating my lips in sticky goodness, the ball of maple taffy softens and stretches, melting in my mouth. I swear my eyes are rolling back in my head.

"I think you like *pigiwizigan*," Chiki says, her gap-toothed grin a sticky mess.

I'm still sucking on the bare twig by the time their mother calls the girls in to help with the meal. Grandfather settles on the stump with me. We sit in silence for a while until Mahingan shows up from his hunting, then Grandfather tells us each to pick up the great snow boulders someone has left beside the camp.

"Follow me." He strolls into the woods, hands behind his back, while Mahingan and I grunt and labor with our boulders, trying to keep up. After about an hour, he stops, then, and faces us.

"Our ways teach us that when a boy reaches his twelfth winter he is taken by his father to a place of visions. Alone there, he goes on a solitary quest. He faces hunger and thirst. Loneliness. Darkness. He faces all that he most fears." Grandfather Wawatie pauses, thinking deeply on each word he speaks.

"I have taken this quest, *Mishomis*, last summer," Mahingan says. "You brought me there yourself."

"For days the boy must stay there," the old man continues, "away from all he knows, to face all that he doesn't. It is not easy. Many are not successful in their quest. Even after a few times, not every boy learns his true purpose. His true self."

Mahingan lowers his gaze.

Grandfather Wawatie glances at me from under his thick white brows for a moment. "But not every boy has such a strong animal spirit to guide them as you both do."

Mahingan looks at me, then back at his grandfather. "Him? Are you saying he has done the quest?" His voice is rising and he struggles to keep hold of the boulder. "He is not even one of us. How can he—"

A look from his grandfather silences him.

Grandfather Wawatie is right. I don't know the *Anishnaabe* way, but I have been on a quest of my own—alone, without food or family. Afraid of the dark. Of the cold. Of starving. Afraid of the *Windigo*. I faced all kinds of fears out here in these woods. I learned who I was and where I came from. But one thing still remained unanswered: *what now?*

"Every person travels their own road, Mahingan," his grandfather continued. "Our paths cross for a while and we walk together. We learn from each other."

"I have nothing to learn from him," Mahingan says, glaring at me.

Sighing, Grandfather Wawatie sits on a fallen oak. "What about you, Jack?"

"I learned not to turn my back on Mahingan Wawatie," I say, meeting Mahingan's burning look. "Chiki told me about your skill with the bow. You shot me on purpose!"

"Of course, I did," Mahingan says, rolling his eyes at me like I'm some idiot. "You were in the way!"

"So you shot me?!"

"I wasn't going to let some *shognosh* get in the way of my bear kill. I saved your life—you should be thanking me."

I'm seething, so I am. Look at him—that smug face. The boulder shifts in my mittens and I lift it with my knee, trying to get a better grip. I still don't know why he's made us carry these all the way out here, just to ask us these questions.

"One last thing remains before a boy becomes a man," Grandfather Wawatie says. "An act of courage."

"Isn't killing a bear courageous enough?" Mahingan blurts. I have to agree. Just facing it took more courage than I ever thought I had.

"You have each met fears in the world around you." Grandfather Wawatie waves his hand at the woods before us, then raises one finger and points to his chest. "Have you the courage to face the ones in here?"

He picks up two handfuls of snow and holds it in front of Mahingan. "Anger," he says, adding it to Mahingan's boulder.

He turns to me and scoops another two handfuls. "Guilt." He sticks it to the weight in my already aching arms. Then, without another word, he turns and leaves us alone with our burdens.

CHAPTER 49

We stand there as Grandfather Wawatie's footsteps crunch into the silence. Are we supposed to wait here? Follow him? I don't think I can carry this great snow ball around much longer. It weighs a ton.

"Anger?" Mahingan scoffs and drops his boulder. It crumbles on impact. "I don't have anger."

I almost have to laugh, but the look he gives me makes me think otherwise.

"Well ... if I am angry—and I'm not saying I am," he picks up a piece of his broken boulder and adds it to mine, "it's your doing. You stole my rabbit."

"Are you still on about *that*?"

"Feeling guilty?" he taunts. I throw the boulder down, relieved to be free of it.

"No," I snort. "He got your anger spot on, but I've no idea

why he says I'm burdened by guilt."

"Oh, I'm sure you've done some stupid things, *shognosh*. Think hard."

"What do you know?" I start walking in Grandfather Wawatie's footsteps. I don't need to stand around and let Mahingan take shots at me.

He runs along beside me. "It wouldn't surprise me if your dumb actions got people hurt ..."

Now 'tis my turn to glare at him.

"... or even killed."

I stop dead in my tracks. "Shut your gob, Mahingan Wawatie. You don't know anything about anything."

"You did, didn't you?" A grin spreads across his face. I want to wipe it off with my knuckles. "I knew you were an *ininigoban*, but, still, killing someone?"

I lunge for him and ram him into the oak before toppling him to the ground. Straddling him, I let my fists fly, hitting his face, his side, anything I can get at. "He wasn't supposed to die!" I scream. "He wasn't!"

Mahingan squirms beneath me and bucks me off. The force of it crashes my face into the oak as I land on all fours, but Mahingan's on me before my head clears. "It's your fault—" he pummels my head with both fists and I raise my arms for protection. "You killed him, *shognosh*, you killed him!"

"I didn't mean to!" I cry. "I didn't mean it ... I'm sorry!"

Something in me breaks, not from Mahingan's fists but from my words. I lower my arms.

He's right. I did kill Mick. 'Twas my fault. Why should I get to live when Mick doesn't? When Da doesn't?

Mahingan's fists are relentless, but a part of me revels in the pain. I deserve it, after all.

"Why did you come here?" Mahingan yells. "Why couldn't you Irish just stay where you were? Maybe then my father would still be alive."

His father?

I'm seeing stars by the time the last of Mahingan's punches hit, my eye is near swollen shut and wet with blood, sweat, and slush. But through it all, I see something I never thought I would. Mahingan's crying. With a final shove to my chest, he crawls off.

It takes me a few minutes for the sky to stop spinning; when it does, I sit up and put a handful of snow on my burning brow. My lid is fat and pinched shut. I spit red and wipe my mouth on my sleeve. Mahingan sits with his back to me, sniffling.

"What are you looking at?" he says, his voice low.

"I'm just checking to see if I got in even one punch."

Mahingan turns. His cheek is swollen, lip cut, and one eye has a purple ring beneath.

"Not bad," I say, wincing as my grin hits my cheek.

We sit there in the snow until our breathing calms and the chill cools our tempers. Finally, I have to ask. "What was that you said about your father?"

Mahingan's eyes flash at me, but there's no fight left in him. His voice is low. "He caught some sickness you Irish brought over last summer."

I know it well. Hadn't I the fever myself? Hadn't I lost my own mother to it? "Typhus?"

Mahingan nods. "He sometimes traded at the Bytown Market. I guess he caught it there."

"I'm sorry for your loss," I say. For what can you tell someone who's lost their father? "I miss my father, too."

I throw down the bloody snow and take another scoop against my eye. "Did he teach you how to fight?"

"Yes."

"Well, he surely did a great job of it."

We start the long walk back to the cabin. Along the way, we talk about the men who were our fathers. The men, in truth, we long to become. We brag about their strength, tell their stories; we share their favorite jokes. By the time the cabin comes into view 'tis as though our fathers are walking there with us, they seem so real. So alive.

"Mahingan!" his mother exclaims as she takes in the sorry state of us, battered, bruised, and bloodied. "What happened to you? Just look at your lip!" She takes his face in her hands. "And your cheek!"

She lifts my chin and winces. "And that eye!"

His mother rolls her eyes and shakes her head. "You do not look like the two boys that left here a few hours ago."

I look sideways at Mahingan, but this time he doesn't scowl at me. In fact, he smiles.

CHAPTER 50

*T*he old wagon rattles and rumbles along the country road, leading me and Da back home. Da lets the reins hang loose in his callused hand, for Squib knows the way well enough. As the winding road crests Killiskey hill, Da stops the wagon for a minute. He takes off his cap and looks around.

"Did you ever see anything so beautiful in your life, boy?" Da breathes it all in, holds it deep in his core. We've been up here a thousand times—'tis the same old road. But to Da, each trip here is like his first. Like he's never seen the hills that roll around us, a great rumpled quilt of patches green and gold, or the mist from the morning's rain rising from the furrows, or the miles upon miles of winding walls that rim the fields.

"Did you know your great grandfather and his before him built that very wall—"

"Stone by stone. Yes, Da. You told me," I interrupt. Why is

he talking about this? Doesn't he know my heart is breaking?

"Do you have to go, Da?" I say, my voice low.

"You know I do," he answers. He's been working summers in the fields of England for as long as I can remember. Most of the laborers head over, for there isn't work to be had here. Potato beds seeded, they'll pack up and cross the Irish Sea for summer work. 'Tis the way of things.

"Can I go with you?" My question hangs between us for a moment. I'd give anything to join him. Mick's older brother was going—why couldn't I?

"I'm sorry, lad," he says, like I knew he would.

My shoulders droop and I pick at the sliver in the wagon bench.

"I'd love for you to come … but I need you here," he adds.

At first I think he's joking—but when I look up, his eyes are right serious. "While I'm gone, you're the man of the house." He holds out his hand to shake. "Can I depend on you?"

I think about what he's asking. 'Tis no small thing. I chew on my lip, deep in thought, as I weigh the burden. Finally, I squint up at him. "Can I still go fishing with Mick?"

He laughs. "Of course—just let your mam know. She'll be man-of-the-house while you're out."

We shake on it. It always amazes me how small my hand feels in his.

"So you'll do it, then?" he says. "You'll watch over my girls?"

I think of Mam, Kit, and wee Annie. "Well now, what sort of Byrne would I be if I didn't take care of my own?" says I. If he's told us once he's said it a million times.

"You're a grand lad, Jack. There's no mistaking that. I'm right proud of you." He claps my shoulder as he hands me the reins. I snap them on Squib's gray hide, clicking my tongue to make him trot.

"Come on, son," Da says as the wagon moves on. "'Tis time to be going home."

CHAPTER 51

Something changed in me after the fight with Mahingan. After Da's words. I know now I can't stay here. I have to move on. For the sake of my family, I have to.

I find him around the back of their shelter, stoking a small fire by a birch-bark canoe that he has upturned and settled on two logs propped in the melting snow. Squatting by the boat, he smoothes the white-gray sheets with his bare hand, examining every dash and dot patterning the papery bark.

"Grandfather Wawatie," I say, sitting on a nearby log. "I dreamt of my father last night."

He doesn't reply as he runs his finger along the seams where one bark strip meets another. Instead, he picks up a billy can heating by the fire and stirs. The clean scent of spruce wafts from his can as he dabs a bit of the sticky, hot goo over a buckled seam.

"He told me to take care of the family. He always taught us a Byrne takes care of our own," I continue. "I guess that's why he worked so hard for his family—even if it cost him his life. And why Mam left Ireland—even if it cost hers. They sacrificed so that we could have a better life. I understand that now."

He stirs the can and moves to the tip of the canoe, but I know he's listening.

"It is time, Grandfather Wawatie. I have to find my sister, Kit," I explain. "I have to tell her what mistakes I've made and hope that she'll have it in her heart to forgive me."

He finishes mending the seam and looks at me, then. "And if she doesn't?"

I swallow. I've thought of that—can't stop thinking of it, truth be told. "That is her choice. But I have to at least try to set things right between us. She is my family."

He considers this for a moment and then, stirring his billy can once more, daubs spruce gum on one last brown dot. "Even the tiniest hole left too long will eventually destroy the whole boat." He looks at me then. "But often the littlest amount of spruce gum is all that is needed," he says. "It is good that you want to patch up things with your sister. Very good."

I smile. "So you'll help me, Grandfather Wawatie? You'll show me how to get to Bytown?"

He smirks. "Why do you think I'm fixing your canoe?"

CHAPTER 52

That night, my last night at the Wawatie camp, Grandfather Wawatie has a farewell feast in my honor. I'm surprised Mahingan showed up; maybe he's just that hungry. I barely make it in time; I had an errand to run first. After we eat, I ask Grandfather Wawatie if I can say a few words. He nods and I fetch the loaded toboggan I'd dragged back from Skinner's place, piling armload after armload of animal skins in the middle of the group. Fox, wolf, beaver, otter, rabbit, and others I don't recognize. The way Mahingan's mother gasps makes me think these are quite valuable, after all.

"I want to give you what is yours—" I say. "Some of these came from your traps."

Kijick and his brother exchange questioning looks.

"The trapper," I explain, "William Slattery, he stole them.

But those others he caught himself and these last few were cleaned and stretched by me."

"Miigwech," Grandfather Wawatie says. "Thank you, Jack."

"No, thank you." I look around the circle at their faces warmed in the fire's glow. "You've welcomed me into your home. You shared your stories with me and helped me to remember mine. I learned a lot in my time in the bush; I even learned how to trench a beaver dam and walk on snowshoes."

"Me, I think you need a few more lessons," Mahingan mumbles, and his cousins laugh.

I look at Chiki and Anami. "I learned how to make bannock, catch sugar water, and roll maple taffy." I turn my gaze to the fire and think of my time in Skinner's shack. "I learned that everyone has a story ... and that sometimes there's hurting before there's healing." I think of how I miss Da and Mam, of what I did to Benoît, to Mick, to Annie and Kit. My voice lowers as I finish. "... and I learned that the things I'd rather forget are the ones I must always remember. For the worst mistake is not learning from my mistakes."

Slipping off my belt, I stroke the simple carvings that run between the paw prints of wolf and bear, over the notches of days, the beaver and ax, DUNBRODY and JACK. "You helped me to remember my stories." I stop at the newly added feather that I'd carved that afternoon. "You are all a part of my story now."

"*Mishomis*, can I say something?" Mahingan asks. The old man nods and Mahingan clears his throat.

I wonder if he's going to tell them about all my mistakes, how I stole his rabbit, their rabbit, and tried poaching in their fishing hole. For stealing from Mahingan is truly the same as stealing from their mouths.

"For twelve winters, I have heard how the white man cheated our people out of their hunting grounds. How the white man destroys the land and waters. How they brought sickness, and still do; my own father died of a white man's disease. I swore I would hate them all."

An unease settles in my stomach and I glance down at the belt, the wolf and bear at opposite ends.

"And when I met you, *shognosh*," he continues, his eyes burning into mine, "I hated you for everything that every white man did to my people. You came on those ships of fever. You worked in one of the lumber camps that take our trees and ruin our rivers. You stole my rabbit."

I swallow. He's right. I did all of those things. And more.

He pauses and the silence is as heavy as the melting snow.

"*Mishomis* kept making me help you ... teach you ... work with you. Why must I do this? I wondered. Does he not know how much anger I have for this *shognosh?*" He turns to his grandfather. "But that is why you did it."

His grandfather's face is like stone, but his eyes soften.

Mahingan stands and walks over to me. "Show me your father's knife."

Unsure of exactly what he has in mind, I slowly pull it from my pocket and hand it to him. I wonder if he's planning on skinning me right here and now.

"I did not want our paths to cross. But I have learned from you, too, Jack Byrne," he says. "You cannot fish or kill a beaver. You cannot snare a rabbit or even walk on snowshoes very well, but you listened to our stories. You honored our way, even though it was not your own. You taught me that all white people are not the same, after all." He shoves the knife blade into his other fist and I realize as he opens it that it holds a leather sheath. Perfectly made to fit my knife, the hand-stitched leather is rimmed with a fine fringe and embroidered with tiny multicolored beads sewn in four small circles around a larger oval. A paw print. A wolf print. I look at Anami and she blushes.

"I cut the fringe!" Chiki brags.

"Now it is a knife worthy of a great son," Mahingan says with a smile as he hands it back.

I slide the sheath onto my belt and buckle it, noticing for the first time that in a circle the wolf and bear prints meet.

Grandfather Wawatie rises and comes to stand before us both. He's got his bowl—a smudge bowl, Chiki had called it. Once again, he wafts the sweet-smelling smoke over me with his feather, and I feel as though 'tis his very blessing settling upon me. He does the same to Mahingan. Grandfather Wawatie sets down his bowl and, taking Mahingan's face in his hands, they touch foreheads for a few moments.

"Mahingan," his grandfather says. "I see you, son of my son." He lays the shining knife in Mahingan's open hands. "Take this now. You do your father proud. You are a son worthy of a great knife." Mahingan's mother wraps a blanket around his shoulders. "Your own blanket," she says. "A sign of your independence. But one with three corners to remind you that you will always need and always have your mother's love."

Grandfather Wawatie places a necklace over Mahingan's head and settles the charm over his heart. "For your courage, inside and out."

Mahingan is right glowing, so he is. And I don't blame him. He did it. A great hunter and provider for his family—a man in his grandfather's eyes. I'm so proud of him I could burst.

Grandfather Wawatie turns to me and takes my head in his hands. He rests his wrinkled forehead on mine and I close my eyes. "I see you, Jack Byrne. I know you. You have learned the lessons of loyalty and truth from a great Teacher—the Wolf. You are kin to this animal who is forever faithful to his pack."

I smile. For he does know me. He always has.

Mahingan's mother wraps a blanket over my shoulders. "To shelter you wherever you go." She gives them a squeeze. "Always remember, a mother's love never dies."

I feel my eyes burn. 'Tis as though Mam is standing there with me, whispering in my ear.

Grandfather lifts a necklace up in front of my face and I see then what hangs from it. A great bear claw, just like the one on Mahingan's. "For your courage, Jack." Kijick hands him a paddle, which he places in my hands. "We wish you safe travels. Perhaps the currents will bring you this way again sometime."

I hold it in my hands and smile at the wise man. "I hope so, too."

CHAPTER 53

"Stick to the shoreline," Grandfather advises as we approach the canoe beside the cabin. "And if the waters are too white, get out and portage."

"That means carry the canoe," Mahingan instructs. "But hold it by the middle or it will tip."

I didn't know it was going to be a lone trip. I thought someone was coming with me. Mahingan, even. Like the few times that we've been out practicing. "But your canoe ..." I argue.

"*Mishomis* can build another like this in a day," Mahingan brags, hoisting up the bow as his grandfather lifts the stern.

Like it or not, I'm on my own for this adventure. The craft is twelve feet long, at least. And they mean for me to man it and carry it single-handedly? But as they rest it upturned upon my shoulders, I realize how light it truly is. We trudge through the woods to the river's edge. *Kitchi Sibi* they call it. *The Great River.* And it surely is. With the warmer weather and melting snow, the sparkling current is surprisingly strong and deep.

"I thought it was called the Ottawa River," I say. For I recall the loggers talking of it.

"A *shognosh* name," Mahingan says.

"They named it after the Odawa," Chiki adds, and giggles. "But everyone knows this is Algonquin territory. Well, everyone except the man who made that map."

Kijick and Mahingan wade in and hold the boat steady as I step aboard. The narrow hull wobbles beneath my weight and I teeter, circling my arms to get my balance.

"Sit down, Jack!" Chiki scolds. "You act like you've never been in a boat before."

Remembering my teaching, I kneel near the middle of the canoe. "Sure, didn't I cross the great sea? I spent eight weeks straight in a boat." I don't tell her 'twas nothing like this one.

Mahingan chuckles beside me. He knows well enough.

What am I thinking? I've never canoed anywhere on my own, and here I'm about to go down a raging river in a bit of bark and sap. Me—that can't swim. I must be mad.

"You'll be fine," Mahingan says, in my ear. "You know what to do. Stay low. Balance your weight. Let the river do the work."

Anami passes me a bundle for the journey: my blanket,

a flint, her hatchet, some dried strips of meat and bannock, and a few pieces of maple sugar wrapped in small birch-bark cones. "Good luck, Jack. Find Kit and bring her back to meet us."

"I will," I say, my cheeks burning in the warmth of her smile.

Kijick hands me the paddle. I think of asking for another one to use the pair as rowing oars, but I do as he tells me and dip the broad end down the side of the boat. Kijick and Mahingan let go and the canoe bobs free. I furiously churn the water on the right side, like Mam whisking egg whites, but all I manage to do is spin in a circle like an old dog readying itself for a nap.

"Both sides!" Chiki calls from shore, repeating Kijick's instructions. "Stroke-stroke-switch ... stroke-stroke-switch," she mimes the action and I follow suit.

"You paddle as well as you snowshoe," Mahingan yells and I can hear them laugh. I have to laugh myself, for I've the sailing skill of a leaf in a gutter.

"Stroke-stroke-switch," I mutter, dragging the dripping paddle across from one side to the other as the boat zig-zags forward. "Stroke-stroke-switch."

"Do not worry," Mahingan yells one last time, his voice skimming across the rippling waters of the *Kitchi Sibi*. "If a piece of driftwood can make it from here to Bytown, there is still hope for you, Jack Byrne."

As I shift my stroke from side to side, the canoe straightens and merges with the current. *I'm doing it! I'm doing it!*

I turn to Grandfather Wawatie and smile, lifting my paddle overhead in a salute. He raises his hand in reply. And so does Mahingan. I wonder if I'll ever see them again and, fearing I won't, I hold them in my sight for those few seconds: a family framed by thick spruce and bare birch, where they proudly stand on the disappearing shore.

The current carries me forward, faster and faster, as the trees whip past. I smile. After all this time, I'm finally going home. For if the Wawaties taught me anything, 'tis that home is neither log nor land, but the people that we love.

A yip echoes from the river's edge. I know it's him before I see his creamy fur, his golden gaze watching me from the top of the rocky cliff. Raising his snout, he howls long and true. Once. Twice. But the third one isn't his. For other wolves have answered his call. He perks his ears and, with one last look at me, disappears into the forest.

We are lone wolves no more. With renewed strength I settle into my small canoe, minding my balance, following the rhythm of the Great River. I will find Kit and Annie. I promised my da I'd take care of his girls.

And that is a promise I mean to keep.

EPILOGUE

I approach the front door of the small, white clapboard house. It surprised me how easy it was to find her. I'd no sooner pulled my canoe up onto the wooden dock and asked the girls washing clothes in the river if they'd knew of Kathleen Byrne. *She's in the hospital,* they'd said and sent me here.

Dear God, I hope she's all right.

I knock. A black-robed nun opens the door. Settling her wire-rimmed glasses back upon her nose, she inspects me. I'm surely a right mess after my long journey down the river. Slipping my hat off, I twist it in my hands. "I'm looking for a girl." I clear my throat. "I'm looking for my sister—"

"Jack? ... JACK!" A clatter behind the nun makes her turn and stand aside. Next thing I know, a body bursts through the doorway, knocking me back into the slush.

I can hardly catch my breath as Kit, my Kit, squeezes the

life out of me. "It *is* you. It's *really* you!"

Whatever words we said at Grosse Isle are long forgotten and forgiven, thank the Lord.

"Oh Jack, I thought I might never see you again. And here you are!" Her face glows. "When you and Mick—"

"I have to tell you something," I say, pushing her back and holding her arms at her side. She'll not want to hug me after I break the news and I hate to snuff her joy. But I have to tell her the truth. I owe her that, for I know how much Mick meant to her.

"There was an accident on the river ... and it was ... well, it was all my fault." I let go of her and look down at my feet. "I did something stupid and Mick rescued me ... only he ... he didn't make it."

My eyes burn and grow wet. I don't think I'll ever get over this. But at least I've admitted the truth. Much as I hate to, I've owned it.

"Oh, Jack," her eyes fill with tears, too. "You think—"

"He's dead, Kit." I blurt. "And 'tis all my fault. And he loved you, Kit. He told me so himself. I swore I'd never tell you but—"

"But you never could keep a secret." The deep voice behind me catches me by surprise and I spin around to see Mick coming out onto the front step with an armload of firewood.

"Mick?" I whisper, afraid my voice would make the vision disappear, for he's surely a ghost.

"The very man himself," he says, his wide smile cutting cheek to cheek.

"You're alive!" I rush at him, knocking the wood from his grip. It tumbles and clatters around the front step. "You're alive!"

"I had a good nurse," he says, looking at Kit. "Never mind me ... *you're* alive! Benoît told us you'd gone missing after the log drive started. We thought you'd died."

"You had us so worried about you, Jack," she puts her hand on her hip, her tone like Mam's. But it warms my heart, so it does. "Where have you been all this time? Just look at the state of you. What in God's name happened to you?"

I look at them both, my big sister and my best friend, as they stare at me in wide-eyed wonder, brows raised in anticipation. They're hanging on my every word, so they are.

I smile. "Have I got a story for you."

GLOSSARY

Anishnaabe - plural is Anishnaabeg. Anishnaabe is the most common term used for group self-identification among Aboriginal people (including the Algonquin.)

Begob/Bedad - Irish-ism for "I swear to God I will"

Ininigoban - poor excuse for a man

Jaysus - Irish-ism for "Jesus"

Kitchi Miigwech - Thanks so much!

Kopadizi - slow witted/stupid

Mahingan - wolf

Mishibeshi - a serpent/lynx underwater monster hidden beneath the ice that pulls boaters and swimmers to their deaths.

Mishomis - grandfather

Pigiwizigan - taffy

Pikogan - tipi

Pwanawito - helpless

Shognosh - Anishnaabe slang for white man

Wawatie - Northern Lights

Windigo - a malevolent, cannibalistic spirit that grows as it consumes humans in winter

ACKNOWLEDGEMENTS

Thanks so much to:

Peter Carver for being the editor who affirms where I am, the teacher who nudges me to go further, and the friend who celebrates with me along the way.

Richard Dionne, Cheryl Chen, Tracey Dettman, Jim Chalmers, and the Red Deer Press family for your continuing support.

Marie Campbell for your encouragement and guidance.

Alan Cranny for, once again, capturing the spirit of the novel in your cover art.

All Saints Catholic High School staff and students for your inspiration and support. A special thanks to Amy Talarico and Graham Mastersmith for sharing your passion for Native Studies, and to Monique Cyr, my go-to girl for all things français.

My draft readers Elizabeth Tevlin, Tony Pignat, Alan and Peggy Cranny, and Kerri Chartrand. Thanks for venturing with me in the wilds of writing and helping me find my way. Without your wise feedback and insight, I'd still be lost. You are my GPS in so many ways.

Kitchi Miigwech to experts:

Suzanne Keeptwo, Editor, Author, and Native Studies Consultant, and Professor Jill St. Germain, History Department of Carleton University. Thank you for being such faithful stewards of story and culture, for teaching with historical integrity and passion, and for helping this story ring true.

Stephen Augustine, Curator at the Museum of Civilization, Stephen McGregor, Kirby Whiteduck, and Web sites www.thealgonquinway.ca and www.anishnabenation.ca for your detailed resources on the Anishnaabeg.

A heartfelt thanks to Tony, Liam, and Marion for all you do during my work-in-progress and everything you are in my life-in-progress. I love you guys.

he previous two novels in this sequence have a girl, , as the main character. This one focuses on Jack, her nger brother. Did you have a particular model in mind the boy, as you developed his character?

k has always been a "right scallywag," as my mom would y. I loved writing his antics in *Greener Grass*, as seen by his aggravated older sister. *Timber Wolf* gave me the chance to climb into Jack's personality and see the world through his eyes. Jack is impulsive, competitive, adventurous beyond his abilities, and yet unsure of himself. He's not based on any one person in particular, but having taught kids this age for a few years, I've known a Jack or two.

You've chosen to have Jack meet an aboriginal family as he tries to discover who he is. How much research did you have to do to make sure that you represented this family with the right degree of historical accuracy?

Though I grew up in Ottawa, I am ashamed to admit I knew little of First Nations' culture. To portray Mahingan's family life as realistically as I could, I did research. A lot of research. It sounds like work, but it was fascinating. I read everything I could get my hands on about First Nations, both fiction and non-fiction, by aboriginal authors; I contacted reserves; I

spent many hours at the Museum of Civilization in Quebe
spoke with Native Studies teachers, and met with Hist
Professor Jill St. Germain from Carleton University. E
experience helped deepen my understanding of the Alg
quin people of 1847. I also worked with Suzanne Keept
Well connected to her local Aboriginal community, Suzar
is an editor who focuses on authentic portrayals of Aborig
nal people. Her feedback helped me capture the voice, cul
ture, and world view of Mahingan's family.

You seem to know a lot about boys of this age. Jack is full of bluster, but he also has a conscience that tells him the bluster often leads him into trouble. Do you think this is especially true of boys of this age?

I'm sure we all know boys, or even some girls, who have the impulsive nature Jack shows. Some people learn by thinking things through and *then* acting. Others, like Jack, learn "the hard way" by acting first and then looking back at what worked and what didn't. The "hard way" works, I suppose, as long as they don't drown, freeze, starve, or get eaten by a bear first.

The wolf is an important figure in this story—and ultimately one of the most important guides for Jack. Why did you decide to use this animal in this way?

Because the story is about Jack finally getting his adventure in the woods, I pictured him as a lone wolf. I must have been watching a nature special or something at the time, but the more I thought about it, the more I realized that it's a perfect parallel. They are impulsive and playful. Both go off on their own and eventually realize how much they need their pack. Jack, like the wolf, is loyal at heart. As I was researching, I learned the Algonquin honor their animal guides, and the wolf is a popular one. Mahingan is named after the wolf. He, too, is a guide for Jack.

You have enjoyed telling stories about Ireland and Canada in the mid-19th century. Yet there's a common assumption that young people have little interest in history, in what happened the day before yesterday. As you've met with young readers and heard from them, do you think that assumption is accurate or not?

I get great feedback during school visits and by e-mail and I'm amazed at how readers of all ages are enjoying the series. People that don't normally like history are loving historical

fiction. I know exactly what they mean. When I was a student, I hated history class. It felt like all we did was memoriz
timelines and treaty dates for tests. Boring! But as an adu
I started to read historical fiction and all of a sudden I w
hooked. Because I got to know and care about the *people*
the stories, I became curious about the facts. It doesn't ma
ter if the character is in a fantasy world, in outer space, or ir
the past—as long as he or she is someone that readers can
relate to in some way. Our problems might be different, but
our emotions are the same.

**Is this the last book in this series about the Byrne fam-
ily? Or are there more stories about these characters that
could emerge in the future?**

Kit, Mick, Annie, and Jack are real to me. I really enjoyed getting to know them. In my mind, their stories—their lives—
don't end when the novel closes. Who knows? I may find Annie's voice or Mick's or Billy's and tune in to what tale they
want to tell.